"I Was Under the Distinct Impression We Had Crossed Some Boundary the Last Time I Saw You."

His voice had become seductively soft, and she felt her resolve weakening.

"Then your memory has definitely failed you. I haven't changed my mind about you." But her heart was hammering in her suddenly constricted throat.

"I suppose I'll survive your wrath, Shelley. I must admit that it does have a certain . . . appeal to me."

She was trying to think of an appropriate retort when he reached out suddenly and drew her to him. The sudden contact with his hard frame brought forth a rush of memories that overwhelmed her, and she surrendered with a small sigh to his firmly possessive lips. . . .

PAMELA LIND

loves to work with words and always wanted to be a writer. Her hobbies include sewing, tennis, horseback riding and, of course, reading.

Dear Reader:

SILHOUETTE DESIRE is an exciting new line of contemporary romances from Silhouette Books. During the past year, many Silhouette readers have written in telling us what other types of stories they'd like to read from Silhouette, and we've kept these comments and suggestions in mind in developing SILHOUETTE DESIRE.

DESIREs feature all of the elements you like to see in a romance, plus a more sensual, provocative story. So if you want to experience all the excitement, passion and joy of falling in love, then SILHOUETTE DESIRE is for you.

I hope you enjoy this book and all the wonderful stories to come from SILHOUETTE DESIRE. I'd appreciate any thoughts you'd like to share with us on new SILHOUETTE DESIRE, and I invite you to write to us at the address below:

Karen Solem
Editor-in-Chief
Silhouette Books
P.O. Box 769
New York, N.Y. 10019

PAMELA LIND
Shadow Of The Mountain

Silhouette Desire
Published by Silhouette Books New York
America's Publisher of Contemporary Romance

Other Silhouette Books by Pamela Lind

Past Forgetting

SILHOUETTE BOOKS, a Simon & Schuster Division of
GULF & WESTERN CORPORATION
1230 Avenue of the Americas, New York, N.Y. 10020

ISBN: 0-671-46158-3

First Silhouette Books printing March, 1983

10 9 8 7 6 5 4 3 2 1

America's Publisher of Contemporary Romance

Printed in the U.S.A.

Shadow Of
The Mountain

1

~~~~~~~~~~~~~~

Jane Grant looked over at her daughter warily. Finally, as though she had become aware of her mother's scrutiny, the younger woman turned toward her.

A small sound that was very nearly a sob caught in Jane's throat. The change in Shelley was startling. What had happened to the fiery young woman who had expounded vehemently just the other evening on the injustices that had to be endured by a woman trying to make it in the male-dominated business world? The eyes that had flashed with emerald fire were muted now, the color of a winter sea, and the normally high color had been replaced by a pallor that actually looked unhealthy. Even the long, burnished auburn hair had lost its life.

Guilt and a sense of inadequacy caused Jane to

stumble over her initial attempt to explain her actions of so long ago.

"Shelley, I . . . please try to understand, dear. I always intended to tell you the truth one day, but . . ." She paused, striving for the right words. "After a while, it just seemed that the lie had become the truth."

Shelley merely nodded, unable to say anything. The lump that had taken up permanent residence in her throat grew more constricting. She knew that she should tell Jane that she didn't really blame her—for in truth, she didn't. But in her bewilderment and anger she had to blame someone, didn't she?

Since she possessed the fabled redheaded temperament, strong emotions were certainly not new to Shelley Grant. But never before had she experienced anything of the magnitude of the feelings that had engulfed her when she learned the day before that the father she had always believed had died when she was an infant had been very much alive all these years. And that his dying request had been that the daughter he had never known attend his funeral.

That final request had been the only reason that Jane Grant had finally told her daughter the truth. And now the two of them were flying westward from their Manhattan home to Denver—and then on to the Rocky Mountain community that had been his home —to attend his funeral.

There were so many questions that Shelley wanted to ask that they refused to order themselves in any way, and so remained unasked. For as long as she could remember, Shelley had believed her father to be dead. By the time she had grown old enough to be curious about him, she had also learned that her mother didn't want to talk about him.

So she had concocted in her child's mind a father—big and strong and handsome—and had immediately decided with childish wisdom that her mother had loved him so much that it hurt even to mention him. And she recognized now, with a bitter little smile, that Jane's remark was accurate for her, too. In Shelley's case also, the lie had become the truth. Long after she should have been wise enough to suspect another reason for her mother's reticence, Shelley had continued to cling to her dream father.

And now, at the age of twenty-five, she was forced to confront reality.

But still the sense of unreality persisted, even after they had landed at Denver's Stapleton Airport, picked up their rental car, and begun the drive west to Mountain Springs.

The silence lay uncomfortably upon them, and finally Shelley could stand it no longer. "Jane, what happened? I have to know. Why did you leave my father? You couldn't have been married very long."

Shelley released her words in a rush. She knew that her mother had met her father during a summer college trip to the Rockies, and had quit school to marry him and live there. That Jane, who was Manhattan born and bred, would have been willing to give up the sophisticated city life, was in itself testimony to her love for John Grant.

Jane was silent for a long while, and Shelley tensed with anticipation. When she thought she could stand it no longer, Jane finally broke the silence.

"No, we were married less than three years. Your

father was a drunk and a gambler, Shelley." She said the words in a strangely flat tone. "That's the chief reason I could never bring myself to tell you the truth. His devil-may-care attitude was a large part of his attraction for me—but it was also the reason I had to leave him. I guess at first I thought that if I took you and left, it might shock him enough to make him change his ways. But it didn't.

"I . . . we, that is, left after I inherited some money from my aunt. I knew that if we stayed, John would soon get his hands on that, too."

Jane stopped and both women were silent for a while, each lost in her thoughts. What was happening to the wonderful father Shelley had created in her mind? She saw him slowly dissolving, to be replaced by a sinister character that made her shudder.

"Did he ever try to find you?" Shelley suspected she was hurting her mother with these questions, but she had a burning need to know more.

Jane shook her elegant head. "No, he didn't. All that I ever heard about him came from a friend I had made in Mountain Springs. We corresponded regularly for a few years, and she wrote that John had continued his drinking and gambling. He even lost the ranch that had been in his family for generations.

"After a while, the letters dwindled to no more than a note enclosed with a Christmas card, and I knew nothing more. But apparently at some point John began to turn himself around. Or perhaps he just hit a lucky streak. George Johnson, his lawyer and friend who called about his death, told me that he had gotten the ranch back—and a small mining company besides. And he never remarried."

The silence returned once more, as they drove westward, through high valleys nestled between increasingly rugged mountains. Shelley turned over in her bruised mind the facts that she had learned. Jane's fierce insistence on independence made so much more sense now. Having been forced into dependency upon a man who failed to provide for her and her baby daughter, Jane had emerged with a singular toughness and determination to stand on her own. She had in fact done quite well. Jane owned a highly successful Madison Avenue boutique and was just now expanding into the suburban Westchester market with a second store.

She had certainly passed on to her only child that independence. Shelley's self-reliance had driven off all but a few of the men who were instantly attracted to her striking good looks. Of the few who had persisted, Shelley herself had only been attracted to one—and that had proved to be a disaster. Even now, almost a year later, she couldn't think of Michael without anger. Michael was a rising young corporate lawyer. From the beginning he had seemed totally at ease with her independent nature. And Shelley had been drawn to him for that very reason. They had drifted into an affair and he had asked Shelley to move in with him. She quickly agreed. They got along well, shared many interests and seemed to be the perfect couple.

In the beginning all went well indeed, and Shelley had actually begun to think that marriage might not be such a bad idea after all. But before long, tiny clouds began to appear on the horizon. The household chores that had at first been shared equally began to fall increasingly to Shelley. And, while Michael expected her to listen at length to his problems at work, he was inclined to dismiss anything she had to say about her job as unimportant.

Matters came to a head one evening when Shelley, tired from a long day's work, was cleaning the apartment alone—in preparation for a dinner party for his business associates the next evening. Michael had gone out to play squash. The injustice of the situation hit her with a devastating blow. Here she was, working just as hard as he was, and she was not only expected to clean the apartment by herself, but would then be required to rush home the next evening to prepare the dinner.

She had left the vacuum cleaner standing in the middle of the living room floor, with a curt note attached to it, had packed her bags and gone back to Jane. She would be forever grateful to Jane for her warm welcome—and lack of questions.

Shortly thereafter, Shelley had gotten a small apartment in a nearby building. Michael had tried to persuade her to return, of course, but she had adamantly refused and had nothing further to do with him.

Instead she threw all her considerable energies into the job that meant so much to her. A degree with honors from one of the country's leading business schools had given her the opportunity to work for one of the Fortune 500 companies, and her abilities took her quickly up the ladder. But now it seemed that someone had removed the upper rungs from her particular ladder.

It was this discovery that had brought on the tirade

that Jane had thought about earlier. Shelley had been passed over for a promotion that should have been hers. The position had been given to a male co-worker, with less experience and definitely less ability.

Anger welled up in her once again as she thought about it. She had two choices: She could stay and fight or she could leave and try to find a more enlightened employer. Although Shelley was a fighter by nature, she knew deep inside that she could not win this battle. And worse still, she suspected that she would fare no better elsewhere. It was a depressing thought.

Nonetheless, she was still mulling over this matter when they approached the small town that had been her first home.

Mountain Springs had a look about it that said it had changed little over the years. It seemed to stand somewhere between prosperity and dilapidation, with little inclination to tip in either direction.

Jane pulled up at a neat little red-brick building that contained two offices: the local State Farm Insurance office and the office of George Johnson, Attorney at Law.

"I promised George we would stop by when we arrived. We'll be staying at the ranch, by the way. John has a housekeeper and she's expecting us."

Shelley was eager to meet someone who could provide another link with her father, so she, too, got out of the car.

Mr. Johnson himself, a twinkling portly little man who reminded Shelley of Santa Claus in a dark suit, came to greet them as soon as they opened the office door. He embraced Jane, then turned to her daughter.

"My dear Shelley, you certainly are John's daughter —with that hair and those eyes. And I see you also got your father's height." In fact, the lawyer almost had to look up at Shelley, who stood five foot seven, even in the low-heeled sandals she wore on this occasion.

Shelley frowned, realizing suddenly that she had not asked Jane what her father had looked like. How had she always pictured him? Tall, certainly—but what else? So completely had her childish image of her father vanished that she could not recall it now.

Condolences were made, regrets expressed that Shelley had not been able to meet her father and they left for the ranch, after Jane had extracted a promise from Mr. Johnson to join them for dinner that evening.

As they were turning to leave, he called to them. "Oh, Jane, I almost forgot. Mrs. Jackson called me this morning to ask if it would be all right if a friend of John's were also to stay at the ranch tonight. I said I was certain you would have no objections."

Jane nodded, then asked if it were anyone she knew.

"No, I'm sure you don't. He and John met about five years ago, as I recall, at Dave McDowell's hunting lodge." Shelley noted the brief look of distaste that crossed her mother's face at the mention of that name.

"His name's Deke Jordan. He's from Montana, owns a big mining company up there. That's how he and John got to be friends."

Jane nodded again, and they took their leave.

"Who's Dave McDowell?" Shelley had to pursue the matter as soon as they were back in the car.

Jane's expression became angry as she flicked a glance at Shelley. "He's a rich rancher in the area—and one of your father's gambling cronies. It was at that damned lodge of his that John started to get in over his head. There was always a group of them up there—all of them with more money than your father had. I always doubted that hunting had anything at all to do with the place. It was no more than a private casino."

Shelley kept her silence as they left town on a two-lane road that wound through the mountainous land. The scenery was almost too overwhelming to be comprehended, especially by someone who had never seen mountains higher than the ski slopes of New England. But magnificent though it was, her mind was not on the beauty around her.

She was more than a little upset by the fact that she would have to share her first evening here with someone who had been a part of her father's unsavory past. Her spirits lifted only when they turned off the secondary road into a long drive that was lined with graceful hemlocks.

The house sat unpretentiously at the end of the driveway. Shelley filled her eyes with her first glimpse of what had been her very first home.

It was a simple old two-story frame house, recently painted in white with dark green trim and shutters. But it had a look of solid comfort about it. As they came to a stop before the house, she could see other buildings through the trees.

Before they could reach the wide front porch, the door opened and two figures emerged. One was a tall wiry man in his early fifties, his face agreeably weatherbeaten in the manner of one who spends a great deal of time outdoors. The other was a plump little woman with graying hair, who appeared to be somewhat older than the man. Shelley frowned as she wondered if this were the man named Jordan that Mr. Johnson had mentioned, and she bristled slightly when he focused his steady gaze on her, before clasping her mother's hand warmly.

Jane quickly introduced him to Shelley as Jud Torrance, the ranch foreman, and Shelley relaxed again as she extended her hand.

The woman was introduced to both of them as Mrs. Jackson, the housekeeper. She smiled tentatively at Shelley. "Oh my, you really look like your father."

Shelley gave her a polite smile, but felt an uncomfortable twinge once again. Being told you resemble a father you have never seen was a strange experience.

Jud carried their bags upstairs, then disappeared. Shown to her room, which her mother told her had been her nursery, she sank down on the bed and wished that it hadn't been changed. Apparently the people who had owned the ranch in the intervening years had had a son, since the room had been redone for a boy, with wallpaper showing western scenes and sturdy furniture. She would have to ask Jane to describe the way it had been when it had been her nursery.

Jane announced her intention to unpack and take a nice long bath, so Shelley knew she would be occupied for a while. She rather enjoyed the prospect of being able to wander about the house alone and so hurried with her unpacking.

Then she paused briefly to survey herself in the big mirror above the dresser. Staring intently at the face that should have been so familiar, she found herself trying to imagine it as a man's face. Only the nose didn't fit. But she knew she had her mother's nose—slightly upturned. The square face, green eyes and auburn hair would all have come from her father. Would she be able to find a picture of him somewhere?

She glanced down briefly at the dusty pink linen suit she wore. Jane had bought it for her several months ago, but this was the first time she had worn it. To her mother's great disappointment, Shelley had just never shown much interest in clothes. In fact, if it hadn't been for Jane, she wouldn't have anything suitable for work. The clothes she selected for herself never varied—jeans and T-shirts for summer, and jeans and sweaters for winter.

Then she left the room, filled with a desire to explore her old home, and to find what she could of her father there. As she reached the bottom of the stairs, she could hear sounds coming from the rear of the house and assumed that Mrs. Jackson was busy in the kitchen. She hesitated, then turned right to explore one of the living rooms, or parlors, as they would have been called when the house was built.

Her eyes roamed greedily about the room, committing to memory every detail—several good pieces of antique furniture, a well-preserved oriental rug. The room had an unused look, however, that disappointed her.

Feeling depressed, she turned on her heel and walked across the entry hall to the other parlor. It was furnished similarly and also showed little sign of use. Then she spotted a portable bar in one corner. A quick glance told her it was well-stocked. She moved away, not wanting to think about her father's bad habits.

When she had returned to the front hall, she noticed another door leading from it. She hesitated, then walked uncertainly toward it. By this time, Shelley was very upset. She had hoped to find something of her father here—but it seemed to be eluding her.

Her breath caught sharply in her throat as she stepped into the room. He was here—there was no doubting it. The room had been a sort of office. A battered old desk dominated the room, before which sat a worn but serviceable swivel chair. Tears welled up in her eyes as she looked about the room.

One wall displayed a large aerial photograph of what she knew must be the ranch. A large table stood in one corner beneath incongruously modern track lighting. There were incomprehensible maps spread across the table. The wall behind it held bookshelves, the books being mostly about ranching and mining.

She approached the desk warily. There were some papers scattered on its ancient surface and a well-used pipe in a wooden stand.

And then she saw the photograph. She had not noticed it at first because it lay flat on the desk. When she picked it up, she saw that the old frame had broken in the back.

For the first time, Shelley saw the man who had been her father. There he was, with her smiling mother and a frowning infant with an unruly thatch of red hair. She stared hard at him.

He was indeed a tall man, on the slim side, with hair the same color as that of the baby he held somewhat gingerly in his arms. But he was laughing nonetheless, and even the worn quality of the photograph could not dispel the feeling that this was a man who loved life and laughed at all misfortune.

A slight creaking of floorboards drew her around sharply. Resentment sprang up even as she turned, expecting to find the housekeeper. And that resentment was increased when she saw that it wasn't the housekeeper, but a total stranger. Abruptly she recalled the friend of her father's who was staying at the ranch.

He was a very tall man, roughly dressed in worn jeans and a plaid shirt. Broad shoulders tapered to a surprisingly trim waist and hips—surprising because he wasn't a young man. The impressive head of silvered hair proclaimed that loudly. She had no further opportunity to dwell on his appearance, however, since he advanced into the room.

"Hello, Shelley. I'm Deke Jordan, a friend of your father's. Has Mrs. Jackson mentioned me to you?" The deep voice suited the man.

Shelley replied coolly that Mrs. Jackson had mentioned it. She turned back to the photograph, hoping that he would say something appropriate and leave. She did not offer her hand.

But he walked over to the desk instead. She stepped aside quickly, in a gesture clearly designed to let him know that his presence was unwanted.

"That was his proudest possession, you know."

There was great gentleness in his tone. Shelley glanced up at him, to find him peering at the photograph she still held. Then the dark eyes shifted to her face.

Shelley was stunned. Seen at closer quarters, he seemed to deny the assumption she had made that he was about her father's age. It had been the hair, of course. But the face was that of a much younger man. She stared at him unabashedly.

He laughed then, causing her to look away quickly. "I'm thirty-seven. Premature graying is an inherited trait."

His easy reading of her mind made her even more annoyed, but she stifled it. After all, he had been a friend of her father's, even if he were a part of the unsavory side of John Grant.

"I'm sorry. I didn't mean to stare. But I suppose you must be used to it, since you guessed right away." She tried, but could not make her voice friendly.

He looked at her with a disconcertingly direct dark-eyed gaze, and she found her own eyes locked on the dimple in his chin. It was a dimple, not a cleft, which would have been more in keeping with the rugged features.

"Did you know anything about your father, Shelley?" Once again, his tone was gentle and a part of her responded to that gentleness.

Looking down once more at the picture, she slowly shook her head. When she found her voice, it was small and on the verge of breaking.

"No. Jane . . . my mother . . . told me he died when I was a baby. She had her reasons and I don't blame her, but . . ." Her voice broke off abruptly, as the tightness in her throat made it too difficult to speak.

His earlier remark about the family portrait being her father's proudest possession hit her then. For all that had been bad about John Grant, he had loved his wife—and the baby daughter he had never seen grow to womanhood. How much he had missed—and how much she had missed him.

She turned her face from the tall stranger and tears began to blur her vision, as she stared at the picture. Perhaps her father had not been the perfection her childish mind had imagined—but he had been a good man. She felt it very deeply. But she would never have the opportunity to see that goodness now.

Wracking sobs shook her slim form. When the stranger's hands rested lightly on her shoulders to draw her around gently to face him, she gave no thought to pushing him away. All the anguish that had been bottled up inside her poured forth and she wept uncontrollably, burying her face in the soft flannel of his shirt. She was only vaguely aware of the strong arms wrapped about her.

"Cry it out, Shelley. You'll feel better." His deep voice vibrated through her, making her suddenly aware of the fact that this man was a stranger to her. She pulled roughly away from him and he let her go immediately.

Brushing a hand across her face, she tried to gather her dignity about her once more.

"I'm sorry. Thank you for your understanding. I think I'd better go shower and change for dinner." Without looking at him again, she hurried from the room.

Back in the privacy of her old nursery, her grief subsided somewhat and was replaced by embarrassment. She hadn't intended to break down like that. As long as she could remember, she had been chastised for her tendency toward strong emotion—usually outbursts of temper—and she had been working very hard these past few years to hold her volatile feelings in check. Her mother had always condemned any outbursts and Michael, too, had been uncomfortable with them.

Anger with herself quickly transformed itself into anger with that man—Deke Jordan. If he had just left her alone, it never would have happened.

2

~eeeeeeeeee~

When Shelley came back downstairs, after showering and changing into a simple beige raw silk shirtwaist that her mother had chosen for her, she could hear voices drifting out from the living room. She recognized the male voice as being that of Mr. Johnson.

She hesitated in the doorway, as the older man immediately got to his feet to greet her. She returned his greeting, but her eyes lingered on the other man in the room.

Deke Jordan stood at the small portable bar. He had changed into more formal clothes—brown slacks and a tan jacket, with a printed shirt that was open at the neck. In the soft artificial light, that strange hair almost gleamed.

Two emotions assaulted her simultaneously. The first was a continued resentment of him as a stranger who had witnessed her loss of control. But the second emotion was less well defined. There was a sudden awareness of him as a man. She realized now that she had not made the transition before from thinking of him as a contemporary of her father's, to someone closer to her own age. It was a strangely uncomfortable thought.

"I believe you've met Mr. Jordan, Shelley?" She recognized her mother's best social tone.

She acknowledged that they had met and, in reply to Deke's query, said that she would like a glass of wine.

He glanced briefly at the contents of the small bar. "I'm afraid John's tastes didn't run to wine, Shelley. Is there any mixed drink you'd like?"

Although his statement had been matter-of-fact, Shelley stiffened at the reminder of her father's drinking habits. She asked for a whiskey sour, after noticing that her mother had one.

Shelley left it to her mother to carry the conversation. She was feeling too drained to be politely talkative. At one point, when her mother referred to "Mr. Jordan," the man in question protested.

"Could we dispense with the 'Mr.' and 'Mrs.'? The name is Deke."

Shelley realized that he had been calling her mother "Mrs." and that Jane had not protested, as she usually did, that she preferred "Ms." She drew herself out of her melancholy to consider that, and found that she was staring at him.

But he had turned his attention to her mother, who was asking him about his name. "It's a nickname. My real name is David Kenneth, after my two grandfathers. But it got shortened to 'D.K.' and finally to 'Deke.'"

Shelley quickly averted her gaze, when those dark eyes rested once again on her. Deke Jordan made her very uncomfortable.

When her mother excused herself to go help with the dinner preparations, Shelley felt betrayed—and wished that she had suggested that she be the one to help.

Left alone with the two men, Shelley found herself being questioned by Mr. Johnson about her life in New York. They had not yet exhausted that subject when her mother returned to announce dinner.

The conversation at the table became more general. Shelley felt somewhat better with Deke seated at the far end where she could ignore him more easily. Only once during dinner was she suddenly made aware of her discomfort in his presence.

Her mother had been asked the usual question about muggings in the city, and replied that she had been fortunate, but that Shelley had had a bad incident on the subway. Shelley tried to downplay it for the company. "The mugger wasn't more than twelve years old. He tried to grab my purse."

When she didn't immediately continue, Jane took up the story. "I'm afraid Shelley's notorious temper got the best of her. She's had training in self-defense and managed to knock the boy to the floor and hold him until help arrived."

Mr. Johnson expressed amazement, whether at the fact of the attempted mugging, or at Shelley's actions, she couldn't tell.

"Life has come to a sorry state of affairs when a

young woman has to become an expert at self-defense to survive," he observed, shaking his head.

Without intending to do so, Shelley glanced at Deke Jordan's strong profile, to see a sudden grin lift the corners of his mouth. So he found the thought of her defending herself amusing, did he? She was really beginning to dislike the man.

After dinner, Shelley insisted upon being the one to help Mrs. Jackson in the kitchen, and her mother capitulated.

Unfortunately for Shelley, who wanted to escape from at least one member of the group, Mrs. Jackson was a very well organized and neat cook, so there was very little cleaning up to be done. She was forced, therefore, to return to them, wondering if she could plead tiredness or a headache.

"I never gave it any thought. But, of course, there really wasn't anyone else. . . ." Jane's voice trailed off as Shelley appeared in the doorway. She had heard the shock in her mother's voice and stopped just inside the room.

As before, her mother and Deke were seated on the long sofa, while Mr. Johnson had taken one of the wing-backed chairs. Both men rose to acknowledge her entry, but her eyes were locked on her mother.

"Is something wrong, Jane?" It was a pointless question. The shock was as plain on her mother's face as it had been in her voice.

It was Mr. Johnson who answered her question. "Shelley, I know this isn't the time or place, but we were just discussing your father's will."

Will? Shelley hadn't thought about it. She gave the older man a puzzled frown.

"Your father left everything he had to you, Shelley. The ranch and the mining company—and a small amount of cash. The ranch has a small mortgage, but that's all. And he did specify a share of the ranch profits to Jud Torrance, who has been here for many years. It's an arrangement they had had since John recovered the ranch. There's also a cash bequest to Mrs. Jackson. But the bulk of it is yours.

"Both the ranch and the mining company are profitable, I believe. Deke here knows more about Lucky Lady than I do."

Shelley automatically followed his gaze to Deke, to find him watching her closely.

"The company is profitable, although I had been trying to persuade John to expand his operations—until he told me about his illness, that is." Deke's calm voice was directed at her.

Even in the stunned aftermath of this revelation, Shelley noted Deke's lack of surprise at the news. He must have known of it before she had.

Shelley's mind swam. The man who had fathered her, but who had never been a part of her life, had given all that he had worked for to her. It was frightening—and very sad. She could think of nothing to say, and so kept her silence.

The others went on to discuss different things, as she tried to grope her way back to rationality. Finally her mother's voice drew her back to the conversation that had been eddying around her.

"Deke, I understand that you met John at Dave McDowell's lodge." Shelley heard the disapproval in Jane's voice.

But Deke seemed not to have noticed. "Yes, I

did—about five years ago. It was just after John had acquired Lucky Lady. Since I'm in the mining business, too, the friendship started on that basis."

Lucky Lady. It was the second time Shelley had heard the name of the mining company that was now hers. It had the ring of the Old West in it—of towns that flourished and died, literally overnight.

Later, Shelley lay wide awake in her bed and thought about this cataclysmic change in her life. What was she to do? Selling both the ranch and the mining company seemed to be the only logical course open to her. But she had heard enough of the conversation that evening to know that her father had worked very hard to build the Lucky Lady into a profitable business. And the ranch had been in the family for generations. Its temporary loss had been a terrible shock to him, she guessed. Did she have the right to sell everything that had meant so much to him? She wondered what he would have wanted her to do, and was once again overcome with grief that she had never gotten to know him.

As she stood in the cool, damp breeze the next morning at the small family cemetery on the ranch property, she knew that she had reached a decision by default. She had not known that the cemetery existed, and had assumed that her father would be buried at a public cemetery in town. The others had departed, but Shelley had said that she wanted to remain alone for a few minutes and would walk back to the house.

Pulling herself reluctantly away from the fresh grave with its temporary marker, she wandered slowly past the other graves. The oldest one was dated 1887—nearly a hundred years ago. The names meant nothing—but they were family. Shelley was beginning to understand what kept some people in small, dull corners of the world. A sense of belonging. One could never have that kind of feeling in the concrete and steel canyons of Manhattan. It was too big, too powerful, to belong to a mere mortal.

She turned away from the cemetery and began to walk slowly back to the ranchhouse, just as the sun peeked out from the thinning clouds. Its instant warmth chased away some of the chill she felt.

She would keep the ranch—and Lucky Lady. And she would make her home here. Jud Torrance could surely be counted on to help her with the ranch. And Lucky Lady was a business, after all, and she was trained in business administration. It was characteristic of Shelley to fail to see the consequences of her actions. She had made her decision, and somehow she felt that her father would have been pleased.

As she approached the cluster of ranch outbuildings, she saw Jud, still clad in his dark suit, talking to one of the ranch hands. He came toward her with a smile.

"Business as usual, I'm afraid. Animals don't mourn their masters the way humans do."

They stood quietly for a moment, until Shelley finally looked up at him. "Jud, I suppose that Mr. Johnson has told you that my father left all of this to me, along with a share of the profits to you."

He acknowledged that he knew about it, but had learned it from her father himself before his death.

They stopped alongside a fenced paddock where she noticed the horses for the first time. There were seven of them, all sleek and well groomed. Several fields away were more, and she heard whinnying from one of the nearby barns.

"Why so many horses? I thought this was a sheep ranch."

"It is, Miss Shelley. But your father also raised blooded quarter horses. In fact, you now own one of the best stallions at stud—along with some fine brood mares." His eyes roved professionally over the herd in the pasture. Then he turned back to her.

"The horses were the only thing about the ranch that interested John—your father. He just never had much interest in sheep."

"I used to dream of owning a horse some day," she said wistfully. "But it was an impossible dream. New York is no place for a horse."

"No place for people either, if you ask me," was his blunt reply.

She laughed. "Spoken like a true Westerner, Jud." Then she turned serious. "Jud, I don't know anything about ranching, but if I were to stay here—and keep the ranch—would you be here to help me?"

His leathery face relaxed into a grin. "Miss Shelley, I was hoping you would say that. The Double G has been in your family for a hundred years now—except for a brief time—and it should stay that way. Of course I'll be here to help you. In fact, I promised your dad just that."

Shelley looked up at him in surprise. "Did he think I would stay then?"

He chuckled. "More like he hoped you would. When he told me about his will, he looked at that picture on his desk and said that he had given you his red hair and probably a temperament to match. And I remember he said that since you were his daughter, you would probably try to take on more than you could handle and just might need some help."

Listening to Jud's recollections, Shelley could almost hear her father's voice. And she was very grateful to the foreman, not only for the brief insight into her father's nature, but also for his support. If he had put her down, said she couldn't run the ranch—or even implied that she couldn't—she might have questioned the idea herself.

When they reached the house, they found it well filled. A sizable crowd had attended the funeral, and it seemed that most of them had returned to the house, where a buffet lunch had been prepared by Mrs. Jackson and some women from town.

Shelley now made an attempt to get to know some of the people present. Having decided to stay, she was curious about her new neighbors.

Among those she met were an attractive couple in their mid-thirties. Tom Roper, she learned, worked for Lucky Lady. He told her that he hadn't been there long, but she guessed that he was Jud's equivalent at the mining company. His wife had grown up in the area, and Shelley liked them both.

She was unable to spend much time with them, however, because of her social responsibilities and she didn't learn anything of Tom's plans. Later she saw him deep in conversation with Deke Jordan in a quiet corner of the living room. She told herself that it was natural for them to gravitate toward each other, but it bothered her, nonetheless.

Just after lunch, when people were beginning to leave, and Shelley thought she would have some time to discuss her plans with her mother, Jane informed her that she was going into town to visit the bedridden mother of her old friend. Shelley was invited to join her, but declined, saying that she wanted to remain at the ranch.

What she had in mind was to ask Jud to show her around and perhaps go for a ride. She had brought jeans with her and was excited at the prospect of riding. She caught Jud just as he was about to leave and asked him.

"I'm afraid I can't right now, Miss Shelley. I'm driving over to Silverton to look at some mares." He seemed to be about to say something else, but a deep voice from behind Shelley interrupted them.

"I won't pretend to know anything much about sheep, but I'll be glad to take you riding, Shelley. I was just considering it myself."

She turned to find Deke Jordan standing behind her, looming very large in his dark suit. She had assumed he would be leaving with the others. Since she could think of no reason to refuse his offer, especially with Jud standing there, she accepted, although without much enthusiasm.

A short while later, they were at the stable. "Jud suggested Clover for you, since he guessed that you haven't ridden much." Deke glanced at her as he hefted a saddle in the tack room.

Shelley acknowledged that that was true. After he had saddled the gray gelding for her, he made another trip to the tack room, carrying the gear over to a large stall on the other side of the barn. Shelley wandered over.

"Oh," she breathed, "he's magnificent." The occupant of the stall was a gleaming black stallion, tall and well-muscled, with a white star on his intelligent-looking head.

Deke smiled at her. "He should be. Your father paid a small fortune for him. If I had found him before John did, I would have certainly bought Black Devil myself." Then he gave her a serious look.

"Shelley, don't get the idea that you can ride him. He may be your horse now, along with all the rest, but he's too much for a woman to handle."

If he had said "too much for an inexperienced rider," she would not have objected, even though she would still have disliked his patronizing tone. But her feminist hackles were raised immediately. She narrowed her eyes as he saddled the sleek animal.

"I assume you mean 'too much for an *inexperienced* woman'?"

He turned briefly to her, as he tightened the cinch. "No, I mean too much for any woman, experienced or not." He led Black Devil out of his stall, while she stood there glaring at him.

"That's the most chauvinistic thing I've ever heard. There are certainly women who can ride as well as men—or better."

He calmly handed her the reins of the gelding. "Of course there are. But there are times when riding skill isn't enough. Times when strength is necessary. Or are you going to try to tell me that women are as strong as men, too?" He gave her a hint of a smile as they walked the horses out into the bright sunshine.

"Can you mount by yourself, or do you need help?" His question came just as she was about to make a retort.

She nodded and swung into the saddle to prove it. They walked the horses away from the barn in silence, until she finally broke it.

"Some are, you know."

He looked at her questioningly for a second, then grinned as he realized what she meant. "I suppose so, but I haven't met any yet—and can't say that I'd want to, either."

Shelley had nothing to say to that, but continued to bristle at his remarks. Finally he asked her if she would feel comfortable trotting. Since she could see he had his hands full controlling Black Devil, she knew she ought to say no, but she did want to trot and felt very secure on the tractable Clover.

So they trotted along the edge of a field that was just turning green. She was really angry with him, which was probably what prompted her to tell him about her decision to stay. They had paused near a stretch of woods.

He merely nodded, betraying no surprise. "I guessed you would. But what about Lucky Lady?"

She really hadn't made up her mind about that, but said defiantly, "If I'm going to learn to run a ranch, I can also learn to run Lucky Lady."

His response to that was to turn away from her for a few moments, staring at the woods beyond.

"Well, I'm waiting, Deke." Her hostility was out in the open now, and he spun sharply about to face her.

"Tell me how I can't run a ranch and a mining company because I'm a woman." She glared at him defiantly.

He chuckled softly, both hands resting on the saddle horn, which he contemplated for a moment before responding. "Would it do any good if I did?"

She tossed her head, sending her red hair flying. "Not one damned bit. Believe it or not, Deke, women are running all kinds of things these days. Some of us just aren't content to sit at home and have babies and clean house."

His answer to that outburst was a slow grin. "So I've heard. And whether you believe it or not, I don't disagree with that. But there are some businesses—like some horses—that require a man's touch."

She was stirred up still further. "And ranching and mining are among those, I assume?" Sarcasm dripped from each word.

"I never said you couldn't learn to run the ranch. Jud is a good man, and he'll help you."

"And Tom Roper will help me at Lucky Lady—or are you saying that he's not a good man?"

Deke shook his silvered head. "I'm not saying that at all. Tom's an excellent man." He hesitated for a moment, then finally went on.

"Mining's a complex business, far more so than sheep ranching. That's probably what made it appeal to your father."

Shelley threw him a triumphant look. "Exactly. And he knew nothing about it. But he learned. And so will I—with Tom's help." She paused, and narrowed her eyes speculatively. "Were you hoping that I would sell Lucky Lady to you, Deke?"

He returned her scrutiny unhesitatingly. "I would have made you an offer, if you had wanted to sell."

"Well, I don't. If my father could learn mining, so can I." And she turned her mount back toward the barn.

For the rest of the day and evening, Shelley did her best to avoid Deke—with only limited success. Jud appeared just before dinner and was promptly invited to stay. Shelley felt guilty about using him as a buffer, but was very grateful for his presence.

After dinner she left Deke with Jane in the living room and went into her father's old office with Jud, where he began to explain to her the workings of the ranch. She sat in the old swivel chair that had been her father's and listened intently, feeling an almost uncanny closeness to John Grant.

Finally Jud departed, after reminding her that work days started very early on a ranch, and she was forced to return to the living room. She found her mother and Deke talking quietly, and from the sudden cessation of the conversation when she entered the room, she had a suspicion that they had been discussing her. Shelley had earlier told her mother that she planned to move to Mountain Springs and take over the ranch and Lucky Lady.

Jane had shown little surprise at her daughter's decision, but she had been cautionary. Shelley had shrugged off her suggestion that she might just be taking on more than she could handle. And she had been more than a little disappointed at the lack of support she had received.

"Well, dear, how do you feel about ranching now?" Jane gave her an almost too bright smile.

Shelley shrugged. "It doesn't seem so complicated. At least, my end doesn't. It's mostly record-keeping and accounting, and I can handle that well enough."

"Today the Double G, tomorrow Lucky Lady. She's already well on her way to becoming a one-woman conglomerate, Jane." Deke turned to Shelley's mother with a grin and a broad wink.

Shelley flushed angrily. "Very amusing, Mr. Jordan. You've already expressed your opinion quite clearly."

"And it's fallen on deaf ears, I see." There was no change in his tone.

"Quite. I've spent far too much time around men of your ilk. Let me tell you, it's going to be a pleasure being my own boss." Shelley threw him a triumphant look.

He was silent for a few moments, then seemed to be about to say something. But instead he got up and went to refill his drink from the bar.

Shortly thereafter, Jane excused herself, and Shelley felt betrayed. She didn't want to be left alone with him, but she wasn't tired enough to consider going to bed just yet.

Without Jane's pacifying presence, Shelley fully expected matters to deteriorate quickly. But perhaps because he, too, sensed this, Deke began to ask her about her college studies and her present job.

Shelley answered his questions briefly, very much aware that both of them were straining to avoid a confrontation. And the strain finally became too much for her. She stood up abruptly and announced that she was going to bed. He stood, too, and for a long moment they regarded each other silently from the uncomfortable distance of five feet.

Finally it was Shelley who murmured a quick good night and retreated to her bedroom, where she sat thinking for a while.

What was it about Deke Jordan that bothered her so much? She had certainly had experience with his type before, but she had never let any of them get under her skin the way he did. She finally decided that his effect upon her was undoubtedly the result of the emotional strain she had been under. There could be no other explanation.

They stood at the edge of the small airstrip, near the single-engine plane Deke had flown in from Denver. Shelley had been surprised when Deke had asked her to drive him to the airport that morning. However, she could scarcely refuse his request, with her mother present. So they had made the trip in an uncomfortable silence, made bearable for Shelley only by the knowledge that he would soon be out of her life.

She hadn't really intended to accompany him to the plane, but found herself doing so. He tossed his bag onto the seat, then turned to her.

To her great surprise, he cupped her chin with one big hand and lifted it so that she was forced to look up at him. "Somehow, Shelley, our relationship has gotten off to a bad start. But I want you to know that I'll be here—any time you need me."

Before she could protest, he brushed her forehead with a light kiss. She knew it was only a friendly gesture, but it provoked a very strange reaction in her—a sudden rush of awareness of him as a man.

Confused, she tilted her head back still further to look questioningly at him.

For a moment his dark eyes peered intently into her green ones. And then his hand slid slowly from her chin along her slender neck and across her shoulder.

She had plenty of time to draw away, but she was mesmerized by his closeness and his touch, and gave only a small cry of surprise as he drew her to him.

Panic began to well up in her as his mouth descended, but it vanished rapidly in the electric shock that followed as his mouth closed over hers.

Her body registered the imprint of his hard male form as her soft lips yielded under the sensual impact of his kiss. Automatically her arms moved up to encircle his muscular neck, and she was gathered even more tightly to him. One hand cupped the back of her head, crumpling the auburn silk of her hair, while the other pressed insistently against the small of her back. His tongue made a brief, sensuous foray into her mouth, probing lightly at hers, and sending shock waves through her.

But then, as suddenly as it had begun, it was over. He released her abruptly, with a quick goodbye, and was gone. She backed off automatically as the plane's engine roared to life.

And she was still standing at the edge of the strip when he took off into the blue heavens. Slowly her reeling senses returned to normal. How had it happened? How had a kiss that she knew had begun as no more than a friendly gesture turned into something that left her breathless even now? On what could she blame the feelings he had aroused so quickly? And finally, she wondered about the surprised expression she had seen on his rugged features, just before he quickly took his leave.

His earlier words came back to her now, as she glared defiantly at the rapidly vanishing airplane.

"I'll never need you, Deke Jordan," she muttered to herself.

3

~~~~~~~~~~~~~

Shelley paused just inside the door to her office. She smiled approvingly. Now it looked like her office. It had been painted over the weekend in a warm peachy beige. And the worn brown carpeting had been replaced with a soft green one. The plants she had ordered had been delivered, and someone had made an attempt to arrange them. There was a new light wooden desk and a modern leather chair. Only the ugly old drapes remained—but Mrs. Jackson had the new ones almost finished. Was it possible that she had been here two months already?

She swelled with pride. While she was uncomfortably aware of the fact that she still had a long way to go—both here and at the ranch—she was justifiably proud of her hard work.

She had returned to New York just long enough to

quit her job, pack her belongings and call a few friends. Then she had returned to Mountain Springs to take up residence at the ranch, and throw herself headlong into work.

She spent weekdays at Lucky Lady, and evenings and weekends learning about the ranch. She knew she was working too hard, but she was enjoying it.

She still felt much more comfortable at the ranch than here, at Lucky Lady. While Tom Roper turned out to have surpassed her already good impression of him and was proving to be a remarkably patient and willing teacher, she knew that the other men in the small office merely tolerated her.

That her father had been well-loved by them all had become very apparent to her. Even craggy old Ben Thomas, the operations chief, had been wet-eyed at the funeral. However, since that time, all she had seen in his eyes had been ill-concealed amusement. She knew that he, as most of the others, fully expected her to give up before long. And that, of course, only served to make her more determined than ever to remain.

Much as she hated to admit it, even to herself, Deke Jordan had been right. Mining was indeed a very complex business. Nevertheless, Shelley was not about to accept his statement that it required a "man's touch."

She was still thinking unkind thoughts about him when her secretary brought in the morning's mail. After dropping it on Shelley's desk, she paused.

"Miss Grant, Mr. Jordan's secretary called just before you came in and requested an appointment with you for Mr. Jordan for tomorrow morning. Your schedule was free, so I took the liberty of setting up the time knowing he was a friend of your father's."

Shelley frowned, drawing a surprised look from the older woman. "What on earth does he want?" The question was asked rather more sharply than necessary and she regretted it instantly, when she saw the secretary's look of dismay.

"I really didn't ask, Miss Grant. Mr. Jordan was a fairly frequent visitor when your father . . . was still here." Shelley noted the slight hesitation and softened. She had begun to half suspect that there might have been something more than the usual boss-secretary relationship between her father and this woman.

"I'm sorry, Julia. It's quite all right." She suddenly felt compelled to explain her behavior. "It's just that he made it rather plain that he disapproves of my taking over Lucky Lady. I'm sure he's coming here just to confirm his beliefs."

The woman's handsome face relaxed into a smile. "Miss Grant, if you need an affidavit as to how hard you've been working, you can count on me. You know how men are—they all think a woman can't possibly run anything."

Shelley relaxed too, sharing in the sudden camaraderie.

"Don't they, though? Well, Deke Jordan is going to be surprised. I'll make him eat his words yet."

But, by the next morning, Shelley was more aware of what she didn't know, than she was of her striking accomplishments. She had chosen her outfit for the day with more care than was usual for her. Silently thanking her mother for all the packages from New York, she had selected a light cotton suit of palest beige, with a narrow blazer-style jacket and a slim skirt, slit discreetly to just above the knee. Under it she wore a pale beige and white sleeveless top. The effect was very businesslike, especially with the neat chignon she had begun to wear at the office. She decided that it made her look older.

She arrived at the office earlier than usual, carrying the new drapes that Mrs. Jackson had finished the day before. With the indispensable Julia's help, she put them up. They both stood back to admire the results.

Shelley had felt guilty at first about changing her father's office. But finally it had been Julia who had cast a disapproving eye about the slightly seedy office, announcing that it badly needed redoing. Somehow, her approval had been all that was necessary, and the work had begun.

Now with the plants adding a pleasant touch and the new drapes that picked up the peachy tones of the walls, she felt that she had created something that was hers. While there was still a lingering sense of guilt that she had banished something of her father's, she guessed that he would have approved.

Working closely, both here and at the ranch, with people who had known him well, had given Shelley an insight into the man's nature that she might otherwise never have gained. And the picture that had begun to emerge was the same as the impression she'd had when she'd seen his photograph for the first time.

John Grant had indeed been a man who loved life—including many of its excesses. No one made any attempt to hide his overindulgence in drink and gambling, and Shelley was strangely grateful for that. But it seemed, in spite of all that, he had been highly respected and well-loved. From Julia she learned that she had inherited from him her outbursts of temper and sharp tongue. Given those particular shared traits, Shelley wondered just how well they would have gotten along.

She was musing about this as she signed some letters Julia had brought her. Tom had been in to say good morning and to fill her in on a few things. But Shelley's normal attentiveness to business was missing this morning. Instead, her thoughts were filled with the upcoming meeting.

She was trying desperately to separate in her mind Deke Jordan the businessman, who was undoubtedly coming here to see for himself how badly she was faring, from the Deke Jordan whose kiss had affected her so strangely two months ago. That she could still recall the moment so clearly troubled her. Shelley was no innocent girl—yet it almost seemed to her that Deke Jordan had been the first man to really kiss her.

And then Julia's voice on the intercom cut through her muddled thoughts. "Mr. Jordan is here, Miss Grant."

Shelley glanced at her slim gold watch. Right on time, naturally. So help me, she thought, if he starts to quiz me, I'll throw him out.

But when the door opened and he walked in, it was the kiss she was remembering.

He was wearing a light gray business suit that was very nearly a perfect match for that striking hair. If Shelley had been secretly hoping that the powerful

45

impression he had made on her at that first meeting had been due to her state of mind at the time, she knew now she had been wrong.

"Good morning, Shelley. Thank you for seeing me." His dark eyes focused on her for a moment, then roamed about the office. "I see you've made some changes."

Determined to be coolly professional, she walked around the desk and extended her hand, suddenly conscious of his overpowering nearness.

"It's nice to see you again, Deke." She ignored his remark about the changes, since she could not be sure he had meant it as a compliment.

He took her proffered hand, holding it just a shade longer than she thought necessary. She forced herself to look up into the eyes that were intent upon her, and had a momentary sensation of something almost tangible passing between them.

"I rather doubt that," he said drily, "but I'm prepared to accept the compliment at face value."

Shelley felt herself beginning to blush at his candid —and accurate—remark. To cover it, she turned back to her chair, after motioning him to one of the two chairs that flanked her desk.

"I must admit that I was rather surprised when Julia said you had asked to see me." She was determined not to lose her businesslike demeanor.

"And you immediately assumed that I was coming to see just how much of a mess you've made of things." His tone was much the same as before. Shelley wondered just how much longer she could control the temper that was beginning to twitch with indignation.

"It did cross my mind." She congratulated herself on having successfully adopted his dry tone.

The corners of his wide mouth lifted in a smile. "I have no doubt of that. But, as a matter of fact, the real reason I've come to see you is to discuss something I had briefly talked about with your father—just before he learned of the cancer."

His dark eyes grew even darker, as he paused briefly. "After that, I didn't bring it up again. And I think he was too angry to remember it himself."

She frowned uncomprehendingly. "Angry?"

He nodded slowly. "Anger isn't an uncommon reaction among people who have been condemned to death. I saw it with my own father, who died of a heart problem. He and John were a lot alike. I always felt they would have gotten along very well."

He waved a large hand in sudden dismissal. "Anyway, I had planned to try to interest your father in a joint venture with my company—in Alaska. We've never been involved in gold mining before, but I've decided to give it a try."

He went on to explain that his father had, at some point, acquired title to a defunct gold mine in Alaska. That had been a number of years ago. After doing nothing with it all this time, Deke had finally sent some people up there to have a look at it. Their reports had been very encouraging.

"It would be a natural for Lucky Lady. My money and your expertise. Or rather," he added with a grin, "the expertise of your people."

If it had been anyone else, Shelley would probably have been amused. But his remark rubbed salt into an already open wound. She stiffened.

"I'm fully aware of what you mean, Deke. And for that very reason I'm not interested in expanding our operations at this point. Until I know the business well enough, I don't intend to undertake any new ventures."

He raised a brow at her forcefulness, but she thought she saw the beginning of a grudging respect. Very grudging.

"Your reasoning is good, Shelley, except that there are sometimes reasons why companies must expand or diversify."

Now he had begun to sound like one of her professors, and she resented his didactic tone. "Lucky Lady is in good shape—and I intend to keep it that way," she said defiantly.

For a moment he said nothing, and she saw a considering look on his face. But then he moved abruptly to extract some papers from his attaché case. "All I ask is that you look over this proposal—perhaps discuss it with Tom Roper. I don't need a decision just yet."

Ignoring her protesting look, he laid the papers in front of her. "Now tell me how things are going for you, here and at the ranch."

She almost sighed in relief. She had faced up to him and won. Or at least she thought she had won. Why the ambivalence, she wondered? Why did she have the feeling he had chosen to be gently persuasive, when he would rather have been deliberately forceful? But his question required an answer.

"Very well. Jud is turning me into a rancher and Tom is doing his best to turn me into a miner. And my riding has improved greatly."

He nodded, giving her that slightly crooked smile that transformed his rugged features into surprising boyishness. "No time for a social life, I take it?"

She fidgeted slightly. "Tom and his wife have seen to it that I meet people, but I'm just too busy to give it much thought."

"Do you miss New York?"

She nodded truthfully. "Yes, sometimes. When Jane calls and mentions having been to the theater or some gallery opening, I have to quell an urge to jump on the first plane and go back there. And I'd give anything for a pastrami on rye." She gave him a rueful smile.

After a few general questions about the business, he rose. "I won't take up any more of your time, Shelley. It's been nice to see you again. And believe it or not, I'm glad you're here."

She, too, stood up and followed him to her office door, wondering why she felt relieved and upset at the same time.

"Thank you, Deke—and I do believe you." She didn't—not by a long shot—but she felt she had to respond to his politeness. His friendship with John Grant loomed large in her mind, as she suspected it did in his.

They had paused near the door and were standing far too close for her comfort. Shelley felt tension gripping her tightly. But before she could attempt to put some distance between them, his hand came up in a repeat of the earlier gesture, capturing her chin.

She made no attempt to pull away, but kept her eyes down, even as he tipped her head back. Her mind was reeling at the memory of his kiss, and there was an unwelcome rush of warmth enveloping her. When she could stand it no longer, she raised her eyes, only to meet his hooded gaze a heartbeat before his mouth closed gently over hers.

This time, however, he made no attempt to deepen the kiss, even though his hand slid slowly around to circle her neck. There was only the lightest of pressure as his firm lips teased her softer ones. But the effect on her was certainly no less than it had been before. Without any conscious effort on her part, her hands came up to rest lightly against the broad chest.

A barely audible moan of protest came from her throat when he released her mouth from its sensual imprisonment. His hand lingered for a few moments longer around her throat before he removed it with an almost abrupt gesture. Much later, when she was reliving those moments, she was sure she had seen annoyance on his hard male features.

But now, after the door had closed behind him, she moved shakily back to her desk on legs that had grown rubbery. Her last thought, before the insistent ringing of her telephone summoned her back to business, was of what it would be like to make love with him.

"Tom, I can understand what you're saying. But I just don't feel prepared to expand our operations at this point." Shelley had begun to feel that this mild argument between them was part of the regular weekly luncheon they shared.

"But, Shelley, you've seen the figures. You read that report. I know that you're still getting your feet wet in this business—but the climate is right for expansion now. And it might not be by the time you're ready."

Shelley frowned into her chicken salad. Tom sounded like an echo of Deke Jordan, who had called her that morning and said much the same thing. She had been forced to confess that she had not even read the papers he had left with her, but she had done so right after hanging up.

She decided to tell Tom about it, and later that day gave the information to him. Two days later he was in her office, Deke's papers in his hand. "Shelley, this is perfect for us. Very little capital committed, and it looks like a sure thing. I think we should do it." His enthusiasm was obvious.

Shelley instantly regretted that she had given him the information. Now she would have two of them badgering her about it. She expected another call from Deke at any time.

So they discussed it at length and, in the end, Shelley remained adamant in her refusal to join in the venture. Tom accepted her decision regretfully.

After he had left her office, Shelley began to have some misgivings. Was it possible that her refusal had less to do with her newness to the business, and more to do with Deke Jordan's involvement in it? If it had been anyone else approaching her with this proposal, might she have looked at it more favorably? She began to mull over her discussion with Tom.

Something was bothering her. It was more than the strongly persuasive nature of Tom's statements, although that he had voiced them so adamantly was in itself unusual. But there were things Tom had said about the project that gnawed at her mind. Perhaps she hadn't read the information that carefully, after all. She picked up the papers again and began to read with singular concentration.

Finally she raised troubled green eyes from her reading. A chill began to creep over her. She returned to their discussion—tried to see another explanation.

But in the end she couldn't. And the chill became a numbing cold, which gave way rapidly to anger. At first she couldn't bring herself to blame Tom. It was Deke Jordan whose image was centered in her mind's eye. She saw once more the two of them deep in conversation on the day of her father's funeral. Perhaps he had been discussing it even then.

Shelley didn't doubt Deke's powers of persuasion. She had heard his name invoked around the office— by Tom and some of the others. And she knew that they considered him to be a top man in his field. She also knew that his company was very much larger than Lucky Lady, and that gave him added stature.

But she was faced with the indisputable fact that Tom knew more about this project than he could have learned from the information before her.

So, for all his friendliness, Deke Jordan had stabbed her in the back. She didn't know at this point if his meddling was the result of his belief that she was incapable of running Lucky Lady, or a sinister way of getting hold of her company for himself. But there was no doubt in her mind that he was using Tom Roper.

Tearing her thoughts away from Deke for a moment, she began to consider Tom's role in this. She truly liked the man and was shocked that he could be involved in something so underhanded as this. Was it possible that Tom was trying to ingratiate himself with

Deke, in the hopes of obtaining a position with his company?

That thought brought to mind something that she had occasionally wondered about. Tom was very good at his work—almost too good. It had occurred to her more than once that he seemed over-qualified for his job at Lucky Lady.

Her glance strayed to the credenza against one wall, where important papers and personnel records were kept. She stared at it for a few minutes, then got up slowly, almost fearfully, and went over to it.

She never even made it back to her desk. The words stood out all too plainly on the single sheet of paper marked "Roper, T.A." And now she had someone else to hate besides Deke Jordan. It hurt her badly to think how she had trusted Tom, liked him. At least, she had never been so sure about Deke Jordan.

It was all there. Tom had come to Lucky Lady only months before her father's death—just as he had said. But what had been left unsaid was that he had come from the Jordan Mining Company. And now, as she forced herself to examine the paper more closely, something else struck her.

His salary at Jordan was not mentioned, but Shelley was astute enough to realize that the executive position he had held there was such that he would have taken a cut in pay to come to Lucky Lady.

Clenching her fists at her sides and taking a deep breath, Shelley strove to control the rage that was building within her. Then she walked purposefully across the office to the door that connected her with Tom's office. The personnel form was still in her hand.

Tom looked up from his work as she walked into his

office. She saw his glance stray from her tautly controlled face to the paper she held.

"Why did you leave Jordan, Tom?" She willed herself to remain calm.

A faint flicker of alarm crossed his regular features, but his voice was still calm. "I thought Jan told you, Shelley. Her mother was ill and we came here so she could be near her."

Shelley knew that at least was true, but she went on, choking back her anger. "Is Deke Jordan supplementing your salary?"

The tension in the room grew perceptibly before he answered, in a resigned tone, "Yes, he is."

She waited, expecting him to offer an explanation. Part of her already wanted to accept it—to believe that Deke had somehow tricked them both. But Tom's silence was eloquent testimony to his guilt.

"Why? So you can spy for him?" The venom poured forth, made all the more bitter by her previous respect and trust.

"Shelley, that's not true. You know that Deke and John were friends. When your father became ill, Deke knew that he needed help here. And he also knew about Jan's mother's illness. So he asked me to come here—to help your father." His still calm and reasonable tones did nothing to deflect her anger.

"Did my father know that you were still on Deke's payroll?"

Tom shrugged. "I really don't know. That would have been between them. Perhaps he didn't. He was a sick man by then and couldn't pay as much attention to business as he once had. But how can you think I'm spying for Deke? Why would I do that?"

Shelley's eyes blazed at him. "Because Deke Jordan can't seem to stop meddling in Lucky Lady—either because he thinks I'm incompetent, or because he wants it for himself."

Tom heaved a deep sigh, regarding her with a plea for reason. "Shelley, I've no idea what he thinks of your abilities, but you're wrong about his wanting Lucky Lady. Do you have any idea just how large Jordan Mining is?"

Shelley brushed off his statement angrily. "I know it's a very large company. But that doesn't necessarily mean that he doesn't want it to be any larger. He told you to persuade me to go along with this joint project when he couldn't persuade me himself."

Tom nodded. "That's true. He did ask for my help. But I agree with him, one hundred percent."

Shelley felt ready to explode, but her voice was surprisingly calm. "There'll be no joint venture, Tom. And you can just pack your bags and go right back to Jordan, because you're through here. I won't tolerate disloyalty."

Before he could say another word, she whirled about and strode out of his office, slamming the door behind her. She did not stop until she had reached her own desk, where she quickly flicked on the intercom.

"Julia, I would like you to call Deke Jordan and get me an appointment as quickly as possible. Then please make my travel arrangements."

She wondered if Julia would succeed in getting her the appointment before Tom could get through to Deke, because she had no doubt that Tom would call him right away.

She sank down into her chair and angrily brushed

away the tears that lingered in her long lashes. If Deke Jordan had been within her reach at that moment, she would have gladly throttled him. Or tried to.

One thing was certain. The feelings that had been roused by his kisses were laid to rest permanently. Shelley went hot with shame over the mere thought of her response to him. The notion that she might have ended up in bed with him filled her with self-loathing. She was certain now that it had all been part of a carefully orchestrated scheme to gain her cooperation in his business venture.

Well, Deke Jordan was going to regret that he had ever tried to pull the wool over her eyes. She would go to him and let him know once and for all that she would not tolerate his presence in her life. The final remark he had made that day at the airport, after her father's funeral, returned to haunt her.

"I'll be here—any time you need me."

4

~~~~~~~~~~~

By the time Shelley boarded the jet in Denver for her flight to Butte, Montana, she could pride herself in having gotten her infamous temper under control. The firestorm of anger had passed, leaving an icy rage. And she was able to admit to herself that her anger owed more to the fact that Deke had almost succeeded in duping her than to what he had done.

She had been very surprised when Julia had informed her that an appointment had been made for her for the very next day. She could only assume that her secretary had gotten through before Tom had talked to Deke. Otherwise she was sure he wouldn't have been so willing to see her. Perhaps he had thought she had changed her mind about the joint project, and was coming to see him about that.

But whatever he may have believed yesterday,

Shelley was certain that he would be fully aware of the reason for her visit by the time she arrived. No doubt he would have some excuse already prepared to explain his underhanded behavior.

She leaned back in her seat with a sigh. Her only regret at this point was that she would be forced to spend the night in his town, since there would be no return flight until the next day. She had questioned why hotel reservations had been made for her in Jordan instead of Butte, and Julia had explained that those arrangements had been made by Mr. Jordan's secretary. She was to be met at the airport in Butte by someone from Jordan, and be flown there in one of the company's planes.

The flight to Butte was uneventful, and she was met as arranged by the Jordan pilot. Soon they were airborne once more.

As soon as she had seen the Cessna, with its stylized "JMC" logo, her disposition had taken a turn for the worse, and the noise and bumpiness of the ride did nothing to improve it. Finally she asked somewhat irritably why they were bouncing around so much, since the weather appeared to be perfect.

"Clear air turbulence, Miss Grant," was the even reply. "We're in no danger."

Finally they were wavering over a single paved landing strip. Almost as soon as they touched ground, she saw the corrugated steel hangar with that same hateful logo. Several other planes similar to the one she was riding in were parked before it.

A stiff breeze caught at her long hair as she stepped out onto the tarmac, aided by the pilot. Shelley permitted herself a small smile as a thought popped into her head: hail the conquering heroine. She was eagerly looking forward to her confrontation with Deke Jordan.

But an hour later, as she toyed with her unappealing lunch in the small hotel's coffee shop, she was fighting apprehension. The pilot had driven her to the town's only hotel, an old but gracious building.

Her first sense of discomfort had come when they had driven past the headquarters of the Jordan Mining Company—a huge modern building at the edge of town. She had known his company was large, but the physical evidence of its size had still come as a shock to her.

While Mountain Springs, her adopted community, seemed at times to be clinging rather desperately to an affectation of gentility, Jordan was obviously a vigorous community that had managed both growth and the preservation of its past. From the pilot she learned that mining had always been its business, and was apparently a very good one.

The evidence she had now of Deke Jordan's wealth and power had unsettled her somewhat. She began to wish that she could have summoned him to Colorado instead. But Shelley was a fighter by nature, and she was determined not to let him or his company overwhelm her.

Several miles away, the man who was the subject of her thoughts was not enjoying his lunch either. The food might be better in the elegantly austere executive dining room, but that made little difference to Deke this day.

His monthly luncheon with the president of the local

bank was a long-standing tradition and generally no more than a social affair, a fact for which he was grateful today, since his mind was elsewhere.

His secretary had reported to him that Shelley had arrived and been taken to her hotel. He knew that the confrontation he had suspected to be inevitable was just that. Why had he allowed himself to be drawn into this? Even friendship had its limits. It had been a mistake not to have told her at the beginning, and Deke Jordan did not like to make mistakes.

Forced to take over the family's business at an early age because of his father's premature death, Deke had shouldered the burden in his characteristically stoic fashion. He had felt the weight of his responsibilities all his life, as the only son and heir of Jordan Mining Company. It wasn't just the company—it was the town. Jordan was truly a company town, in the classic sense of the word. What it meant was that the town's very life depended upon the man who sat in the second-floor corner office.

Difficult and far-reaching decisions had demanded his attention almost from the day he had assumed control, and he took a certain amount of quiet pride in the knowledge that he had made the right decisions over those ten years.

But he was not so sure about a decision made a few short months ago. All he could see ahead of him in that regard was trouble—in the form of a woman with flame-colored hair and a temper to match.

Since the age difference had never been a factor in his friendship with John, Deke had been taken aback to meet the daughter, to find her a woman, rather than the child he had somehow pictured. As a woman, she had to be dealt with very differently, but he knew that he was not handling the situation well at all.

He turned his attention reluctantly back to the banker, then glanced at his watch to note gloomily that she was probably waiting for him in his office.

Shelley had been picked up, as prearranged, at the hotel, and was quickly shown to his office. She was having difficulty maintaining her righteous anger. The place was just too impressive. And that brought reluctant thoughts about just how impressive the owner could be. She paced about restlessly, having been assured that he would be there momentarily.

One paneled wall of the office was covered with expensively framed old photographs. She glanced at them without much interest at first. Then her eyes were drawn to one photograph in particular, which showed a tall man with gray hair standing before the entrance to a mine, above which was a hand-lettered sign that read: "Jordan #1." The date on the picture, hand-lettered in one corner, was 1889. She peered at the roughly clad man in the photo. There was a resemblance there, to Deke—they had the same virile features. This would probably have been his great-grandfather, she calculated. She felt weighed down by all this tradition.

A sound behind her drew her quickly into the present. She whirled about to face the current Jordan.

He is impressive, she thought reluctantly, as she stared mutely at him. He was wearing a light gray suit and striped shirt with gray tie. The absence of strong colors served to accentuate that rugged face and steel gray hair.

He, too, was silent, as his dark eyes swept slowly over her. She had selected a favorite from among the clothes Jane had sent her—a creamy white tailored suit, with a soft coral silk shirt.

"Hello, Shelley. You're looking well." He gave her a pleasant smile, then shifted his glance to the long leather sofa in one corner of the office and a handsome teak coffee table, similar in style to the large desk that dominated the room.

Shelley quickly guessed that he intended to suggest they sit there, and she moved toward one of the comfortable chairs placed before his desk. She did not want this meeting to seem informal.

Without waiting for him to ask, she took one of the chairs, then turned to face him. "I assume your spy has told you by now why I'm here." She saw no reason to be pleasant, and wanted to get the purpose of her visit out in the open right away.

He returned her stare for a long moment, then turned to walk behind his desk and sink into the big leather chair. He tilted it back, and continued to regard her with an unreadable expression.

"I assume you're referring to Tom Roper?" he asked evenly.

She flared, angry that her opening thrust had not provoked him. "You know damned well that's who I mean. Just how long did you think you could get away with this?"

To her chagrin, she saw what appeared to be a genuine smile of amusement flicker across his strong face. "Longer than I seem to have done."

"You mean that you admit that Tom has been your spy?" She questioned him coldly.

"That isn't what I meant at all." His voice was still calm, placating. "I only meant that I had hoped you wouldn't learn of Tom's background. How could I have sent him to spy on you, when he joined Lucky Lady while your father was still alive?"

She said nothing, and he continued. "That Tom went to Lucky Lady at all was no more than a confluence of circumstances. Your father was sick and needed help. The only man who might have helped him run the company had retired and moved to Arizona. And Tom's mother-in-law had become ill, and his wife wanted to return to Colorado."

Shelley interrupted him. "Did my father know you were supplementing Tom's salary?"

He shook his head. "No. If he had asked, I would have told him, of course. But he was a sick man by then, and there was too much on his mind. I did what I did out of friendship for your father, Shelley—no more than that."

For a moment, she almost believed him, such was the power of his persuasive charm. "I can't believe my father would have accepted your charity," she flung at him.

But again he remained unperturbed. "What you refer to as charity, I would call a favor to a friend—as well as a rather practical solution to the problem of losing Tom, whom I consider to be a valued employee. It was always Tom's intention—and mine—to have him return to Jordan."

"That is precisely what he will be doing, probably more quickly than either you or he intended." Her eyes flashed triumphantly at him.

"So I've heard," was his noncommittal reply.

Shelley was fuming. He was taking this all too well. She wanted to see him as angry as she was. "Why didn't you have the decency to tell me about this before?"

He shrugged his wide shoulders. "I almost did, when you told me of your decision to stay and run Lucky Lady yourself. But I guessed rather accurately what your reaction would be. And you needed Tom's help. You still need it."

Shelley curved her full lips into an unpleasant sneer. "How kind of you to save me from myself."

"Are you going to try to deny that Tom has been a great help to you, Shelley?"

She frowned. This was the thing that bothered her most at this point. Tom had been a tremendous help to her, and she knew that she still needed him.

To Deke she said, "I won't deny that at all. But I'll manage without him well enough. I've learned a lot in these past few months." Even to her, it sounded childishly defiant.

From the quick smile that flickered across his face, she knew that he too had recognized her words for what they were.

She hurried on. "I came to tell you that I have decided not to join with your company in that Alaska project. So all your persuasion has come to nothing." She finished with a triumphant toss of her head.

The look he gave her was that maddeningly calm gaze. "Shelley, there are any number of companies I could have invited in on the project—or we could do it ourselves. That I invited Lucky Lady to join us was because I know it would be good for the company.

Now is the right time for a new venture for your company. Surely you can see that just by reading the financial statements."

She exploded. "Are you saying that you've been reading my financial statements?"

He seemed to consider his answer for a moment. "Yes, I have."

She stood up abruptly, and glared at him, green sparks almost leaping from her eyes. "You've gone too far, Deke Jordan. I'm going to see an attorney just as soon as I get back to Colorado. Meddling is one thing, but what you've been doing is clearly illegal. And it will give me the greatest of pleasure to see you pay for it." Her voice was icy with anger and she whirled about to leave his office.

Shelley had her hand on the doorknob and had pulled the door partially open when he gripped her arm firmly with one hand, and closed the door with the other.

"Shelley, come back and sit down. We're not finished."

For a moment she stared at him in disbelief. Gone was the placating tone, and in its place a harsh coldness that she had not heard before.

"You're right about that, Deke. We're far from finished." She pulled her arm from his grasp. "I'll see you in court."

He said nothing, but grasped both her hands in his much larger one and proceeded to forcibly lead her back to the chair. As soon as he had released her, she tried to stand up, but he blocked her way and reached into the breast pocket of his jacket.

"Read this, Shelley." He thrust a single piece of paper at her.

The first thing she saw, with a mounting sense of dread, was her father's signature. She had grown accustomed to seeing it, both at the office and at the ranch. Quickly she scanned the typewritten lines, and the hand that held the piece of paper began to tremble. Ice water coursed through her veins.

Her father had given control of Lucky Lady to Deke. How could he have done this to her? She continued to stare in disbelief at the hateful paper, refusing to look up into the dark eyes of the man she had just confronted. The victory she had so briefly savored turned into bitter defeat.

Finally she did raise her head to glare at him accusingly. "You tricked him into this. I don't know how, but you did."

Deke shook his head. "No, Shelley. You haven't learned much about John if you believe he could have been tricked into something like this."

Then his stern expression softened into one of wry amusement. "In fact, I've just been thinking that he was the one who did the tricking. I think he may have guessed pretty accurately just what he was getting me into."

"Why?" The one word was all she could manage. She knew she was dangerously close to tears.

"He thought there was a chance you might try to run Lucky Lady yourself, and he knew you couldn't do it. As far as the ranch was concerned, he knew that by giving Jud a share of the profits, he could guarantee his help. But he wanted to be sure you would have someone to help you at Lucky Lady. He did it to protect your inheritance, Shelley."

She laughed bitterly, tasting the salty beginning of tears. "So he gave you the company." She forced herself to say the words, nearly choking in the process.

Once again, he shook his head. "No, Shelley. Lucky Lady is yours. He merely gave me control for five years—or less, at my discretion."

She got up angrily then, forcing him to take a few steps backward. Tears were spilling over from the emerald eyes now, and she knew she had to get away from him. But she made one last effort to control herself.

"We both know that will never happen." The sentence held all the bitterness she felt. "After all, I'm a woman, and there are some things a woman just can't do—you said so yourself."

Once again she turned to flee from his office, not wanting him to see her pain. And again she was stayed by a firm hand.

"Shelley," he said, his voice soft now, "I know this is difficult for you, but. . . ."

She pulled away from him. "I don't want your sympathy, Deke. I want you out of my life."

He winced slightly at the vehemence of her statement. When he spoke, his tone was cold and business-like. "Tom stays at Lucky Lady, and I hope I can trust you not to take it out on him. He knew about this agreement, and has just been doing his job. And Lucky Lady will be joining in the Kayalak project." He made no attempt to soften his words this time.

She threw him one last look of hatred. "You're the boss," she said icily.

Back at the hotel, Shelley flung herself onto the big bed and pummeled the pillow in helpless rage. How could her father have done this to her? She was overcome once again with the unfairness of his death. If only he had gotten to know her.

Unfair. It seemed that everything in her life was unfair. One of the chief reasons she had given up her job and life in New York had been to get away from the male domination that had infuriated her in the business world. The prospect of being her own boss had been a tantalizing one. And now she had been thwarted once more.

Not only did she now find herself working for a man who was an admitted male chauvinist, but worse still, she had been attracted to the man in a frightening way. She simply could not walk out on this job—or could she?

As she thought about it, she undressed mechanically and fell into the big bed. She had slept little the previous night, since she had been too keyed up for the confrontation with Deke.

She really had only two options. She could just walk out on Lucky Lady, selling it to anyone other than Deke. She was sure he could not prevent that, so long as she got a fair price. Or she could stay and hope to convince him that she was capable of managing the company.

She ran the options through her tired mind. If she abandoned Lucky Lady, she would be left only with the ranch. And that presented little challenge to her.

But she couldn't bring herself to sell the ranch that had been in the family for generations.

Just as she drifted down into an uneasy sleep, she knew that she had no real choice—she had to stay. And somehow she had to convince Deke that she was capable of running Lucky Lady. But what was she to do about the feelings that he had aroused in her? Even in her anger, she had been all too aware of him as a man.

When she awoke, the room was in shadow. A quick glance at her travel alarm confirmed what her rumbling stomach was telling her. It was dinnertime. She pulled herself lethargically from the bed and went off to the adjoining bathroom, hoping to revive herself with a shower.

A short time later, dressed in the bright green dress that was the only other outfit she had brought along, she stepped into the charmingly old-fashioned lobby. She glanced toward the entrance to the hotel's small dining room. But recalling the less than appetizing lunch she had had in the hotel, she walked instead toward the desk.

After learning that there was a good Italian restaurant in town, she set off to walk the few blocks the desk clerk had indicated. Shelley loved Italian food, but usually avoided it for the sake of her slim figure. However, this night she needed something to bolster her flagging spirits.

To avoid thinking about her problems, she concentrated on the display windows of the shops she passed along the way. She had just about lost interest in this diversion when she came upon a dress shop with exceptionally attractive windows. The professional touches applied here would look at home on Fifth Avenue, she thought with a pang of remembrance. Her mother's Madison Avenue boutique did not look better.

One dress, nicely displayed on a half-mannequin, caught her eye. The color was a perfect match for her hair—a deep rusty red, shimmering with lighter highlights. She paused to peer at it. It had a slightly stiff-looking high neckline that plunged to a deep vee, and the dropped shoulders that were so popular. The sleeves and skirt were full. She decided that if the shop had been open, she would have bought the dress. It was a most unusual feeling for her, since she relied on Jane for most of her dressy wardrobe.

She walked on, thinking that she should have time to return to the shop in the morning, before her flight to Butte.

She found the restaurant without any problems, and was relieved to see that it was uncrowded. It was pleasant and unpretentious, furnished with captains' chairs and checked tablecloths. Delicious aromas wafted out from the kitchen and reminded her of how hungry she was. She had eaten no breakfast and very little lunch.

As soon as she was seated at a small table near one corner, a waitress came to take her drink order. Shelley hesitated. She really shouldn't drink on an empty stomach, but a drink just might help to relax her frazzled nerves. So, without considering the wisdom of her order, she asked for a martini.

When it arrived, she stared at it dubiously. Her drinking was usually confined to wines, and she had never even had a martini. She had heard that they tended to relax one very quickly, so she removed the olive and picked up the delicate glass with determination.

She was halfway through the drink with no noticeable effects when a voice close to her side drew her around sharply. Think of the devil, and here he is, she thought to herself, as she stared up into Deke Jordan's dark eyes.

"Hello, Shelley. I see you found your way to the best restaurant in town. Would you consider joining us?" He indicated two other men who were being seated at a nearby table.

"No, thank you," she replied acerbically. "I prefer to dine alone."

"The men with me will be working on the Kayalak project, and we'll be discussing that—particularly Lucky Lady's involvement. You should be part of it, Shelley. I had intended to ask you before you left my office this afternoon." There was no rebuke in his voice, but she imagined that she heard it anyway.

"This is not my project, Deke. I thought I had made that clear. It's your project, and I'm sure you can run it without my help." She flashed him a withering look that she hoped would send him away.

It worked, apparently, since he left, saying that the invitation stood, if she changed her mind.

Shelley was disgusted. She had come here to enjoy a quiet dinner—and he had spoiled even that for her. She drained the rest of the martini and ordered another when the waitress brought her a dinner menu.

Over the rim of her upraised glass she saw the two men with Deke dart curious glances at her. Shelley suspected that he must have told them who she was, and wondered what excuse he had given for her failure to join them. She considered getting up to change her seat, so that she would be facing away from them, but since Deke at least had his back to her, she remained where she was.

Every time her eyes were unwillingly drawn to their table, she found the men deep in conversation. And it began to bother her that it was her company that was being discussed. In spite of what she had said in Deke's office, she knew that the company was still hers. And she should know what plans he had for Lucky Lady. Her good business sense was beginning to reassert itself. Besides, she thought maliciously, it just might cause him some embarrassment to have her show up unexpectedly. She felt slightly better— perhaps the second martini was having some effect, after all.

Picking up the nearly empty glass, she walked over to the table. One of the others must have warned him, since he stood quickly and pulled out the empty chair for her, after introducing her to the other two men.

She acknowledged the introductions politely and seated herself gracefully, just as the waitress came to take their orders. When the girl asked if anyone wanted another drink, the men all ordered refills. But Shelley, feeling the effects of the second martini, declined.

During the meal that followed, Shelley remained mostly a listener, although she interrupted from time to time to ask a question. Each time Deke answered her patiently. Even that irritated her, so that she stopped asking questions and turned her attention instead to the excellent *fettucine alfredo*.

After dinner, the men ordered brandy, while Shelley asked for a sweet Italian liqueur that was a particular favorite of hers. When she declined coffee, she saw Deke cast a quick glance at her, but she met his eyes defiantly, and he said nothing.

Before long, to her regret, the other two men excused themselves and left her alone with Deke. Shelley toyed nervously with the now empty cordial glass. He had been maddeningly polite and pleasant to her all through dinner. It was unnerving, to say the least. And, considering her still smoldering anger with him, she naturally assumed the worst—that he had taken a paternalistic attitude toward her, and was indulging his old friend's daughter's childish tantrums.

"Are you sure you don't want some coffee, Shelley?" Deke's quiet query drew her sharply away from her thoughts.

Was he trying to imply that she was drunk? She threw him a withering look. "No, thank you. If I had wanted coffee, I would have asked for it."

The waitress appeared just then with the check, and she considered insisting upon paying for her own dinner. But she remained mute. For all her occasional displays of temper, Shelley really didn't like to make scenes in public. And she suddenly discovered she had no desire to contribute to his impression of her as a child. So she merely thanked him coolly for dinner as soon as the waitress had departed and announced her intention of leaving.

She stood up and a slight dizziness immediately washed over her. She was mortified. Why had she had those martinis? She gripped the back of her chair and took a few deep breaths. She was inestimably glad when the dizziness vanished as rapidly as it had appeared.

"Are you all right?" She looked up to find him scrutinizing her closely.

Shelley immediately straightened up and tossed her head defiantly. "I'm fine."

Then, ignoring him completely, she walked hurriedly across the restaurant, pausing just outside the door, grateful for the cool evening air. She felt strangely unsettled. Too much had happened in too short a time—first the news of her father, and now this discovery that she wasn't even in control of Lucky Lady. As she stood uncertainly on the sidewalk, her waist was suddenly encircled in a firm grip, and she was being propelled down the sidewalk.

"Let me go," she said angrily as she tried unsuccessfully to pull away from him.

But he just tightened his grip on her. His voice was very quiet, but firm nonetheless. "Knock it off, Shelley. You've created enough of a scene already, refusing to join us, then walking out without waiting for me. Whether you like it or not, we're going to have some coffee, and talk this over."

Just then, Shelley caught sight of some other people just behind them. Her face flushed crimson as she realized that she had indeed created a scene. She allowed him to lead her over to a gray Mercedes parked nearby, and before she quite knew what had happened, she was seated beside him in the car.

As he started the engine and moved out onto the street, he threw her a quick glance. "Shelley, there's something you have to understand. This is not New York. And while behavior like that might pass unnoticed in a city, it certainly doesn't here. Especially when it involves me. There isn't anyone in this town who doesn't know me—and many of them work for me."

Shelley started to make an acid comment, but clamped her mouth shut. Something in his tone warned her that she had gone just about as far as she dared—unless she was prepared to face some very unpleasant consequences.

So she turned to stare morosely out the side window, and sank back against the cool leather upholstery. I have nothing to talk over, she said to herself. All I want now is to get away from him—and his damned town.

She paid scant attention to where they were going until the car suddenly rolled to a stop in the semicircular end of a driveway. Before her was an impressive old stone house. A light burned over the front door, set under a decorative stone arch.

He got quickly out of the car, but Shelley sat still. It wasn't that she was waiting to be helped from the car—she considered that an outmoded gesture. But she just didn't know what she was doing here. It hadn't occurred to her that he intended to take her to his house.

When he opened her door, she refused the proffered hand, and slid out of the car, knowing she should be ordering him to take her back to the hotel.

She had only a quick impression of a foyer of generous proportions, with a highly polished wood parquet floor partially covered by a deep-toned oriental rug. And then he ushered her into a large living room, where she walked uncertainly to one of two long rust velvet sofas that faced each other, flanking a massive stone fireplace. There was an air of subdued elegance to the room that she could hardly ignore, even in her present confused state of mind.

Shelley shivered slightly in the evening coolness, and he seemed to take note of it immediately. "I'll light a fire just as soon as I get some coffee going."

Grateful for his temporary absence, she curled into one corner of the sofa, absently kicking off her shoes and drawing her legs beneath her. She stared at the piled logs contemplatively.

If only. Those two words seemed to preface every sentence of her thoughts now. If only she had gotten to know John Grant before he died. If only he had given control of Lucky Lady to anyone but Deke Jordan. If only the man weren't so damnably attractive.

The man in question returned to the room then and she averted her gaze from his broad back as he lit the fire. He had shed his jacket, and muscles rippled smoothly beneath the light fabric of his shirt—an unwelcome reminder to her of how it felt to be held in his arms.

"I can't seem to get used to the coolness of the nights out here. It's like this in Mountain Springs, too."

His wide mouth relaxed into a smile. "Having spent a few summer nights in Manhattan, I'd have to say that getting used to this would be a pleasure."

As usual, she felt compelled to rise to the defense of her beloved home. "The weather may be terrible, but there's no place I'd rather be."

"I've noticed before that you New Yorkers are a

defensive lot. I like New York—but only to visit, and preferably in cool weather."

She was saved from having to respond to that by his excusing himself to get the coffee. However, he was back quickly, and after they had fixed their coffees, he took a seat on the sofa opposite her.

"Shelley, as I said before, we have to talk. I know that you're upset about my controlling Lucky Lady, and right now, I can't honestly say that I'm very happy about it myself. But I made a commitment to your father—and I intend to honor that commitment.

"I intend to be as unobtrusive as possible. Day to day control of Lucky Lady is yours, as it should be."

She interrupted him angrily. "Thanks a lot, Deke. Let me think I'm in charge. But if I step outside the little circle of control you've so generously given me, I get stepped on. Isn't that it?" Her eyes blazed green fire at him.

He regarded her quietly for so long that she began to squirm uncomfortably, and smoothed her skirt over as much of her exposed legs as she could. When she at last met his look, it was to find him staring intently at the cleavage exposed by her low neckline. Her hand flew involuntarily to that area.

The movement seemed to have the desired effect, since he looked away from her briefly and turned to the crackling fire. When he returned his attention to her, nothing was written on those virile features.

"Shelley, why is it too much to expect that you could understand your lack of experience? I was about your age when I had to take over Jordan Mining because of my father's death. And even though I'd grown up in the business, and had degrees in mining and business, I wasn't equipped to handle it."

She remained unconvinced, although she was surprised at any admission of inadequacy on his part. "But you managed—and so could I."

He sighed heavily before narrowing his gaze on her. "Exactly what is it that bothers you so much, Shelley? Is it the fact that *I'm* the one who has control of Lucky Lady?"

Shelley stared at him in shocked surprise. So he had guessed her attraction to him? How was she to answer him? To deny the truth in his question would be ludicrous, so she decided to dwell on the other reason she resented his control.

"Deke, I've spent three years working for male chauvinists, and when my father left Lucky Lady to me, I saw my only chance to get away from that. Can you honestly expect me to be happy to find out that I'm now working for another of the same kind?"

A smile played along the corners of his mouth and danced in his dark eyes. "Ah yes. Back to the Black Devil episode," he chuckled, referring to the fractious stallion that had first incurred her wrath against him.

"Shelley, you were an inexperienced rider, and he's a beautiful animal. I did no more than Jud would have done when I warned you to stay away from him. Have you ridden him yet?"

She was tempted to lie and say yes, but instead she just shook her head. However, when she saw the look of triumph on his face, she plunged ahead angrily.

"I just may one of these days—when I get more experience. But you're sidestepping the issue, Deke."

Only when she saw the triumphant look return did she realize that she had walked into his trap.

"Exactly. And when you get more experience, you'll run Lucky Lady yourself, too."

Shelley flung herself irritatedly from the sofa and strode quickly to the hearth. At the moment, she was madder at herself than at him. She had been bested in this verbal battle, and she knew it. Finally she whirled about to face him, hands planted firmly on her curved hips.

"I haven't heard you denying that you're a male chauvinist, Deke. At least my previous bosses paid lip service to equality."

He had stretched one long arm along the top of the sofa, and now cocked his head toward her. Although his expression was devoid of amusement at the moment, she saw dark lights dancing in his eyes.

"Well, at least that proves I'm not guilty of hypocrisy —will you concede that?"

"Certainly. But that doesn't make you any less chauvinistic. How many women do you have on your corporate staff?"

He returned her glare with equanimity. "None, as a matter of fact. Mining isn't a field that appeals to women as a rule, and I hire the best people I can get, regardless of sex."

Seeing that this conversation was getting her nowhere, Shelley said tiredly, "I'd like to go back to the hotel now, Deke. If you like, I can take a cab."

Was she actually disappointed when he stood quickly and offered to drive her back? It seemed that he, too, was ready to end their conversation.

At the front door she made one final thrust. "We're never going to get along, Deke."

He paused, after opening the door, and looked down at her. "For once we agree. But it's just possible we can find some common ground, don't you think?"

"Never," she spat out at him, as she swept past and opened the car door.

But later, back at the hotel, she remembered the intensity of his dark gaze, and knew just what common ground he had in mind. Never, she repeated emphatically to herself.

However, she recognized with a fatalistic sigh that she had to work with him. Having discarded the notion of selling Lucky Lady, she really had no choice. One question he had asked returned to her thoughts now. "Is it the fact that *I'm* the one who has control of Lucky Lady?"

Shelley was as uncomfortable now as then with that question. She tried to imagine her feelings if someone else—say Tom Roper—had been left in control of the company. But the answer eluded her and, in any event, the fact that he had asked at all was more important to her at the moment.

He knew. There was no way around it. Deke knew that she was attracted to him. And she wondered just what he planned to do with that knowledge.

5

~~~~~~~~~~~~~~~

The loud jangling near her ear pulled her reluctantly from the depths of her sleep. Finally her awakening mind recognized it as the sound of a telephone, and she reached for it clumsily without opening her eyes. Only when it crashed to the floor did she finally force herself to awaken fully.

She stumbled out of bed and knelt on the floor to pick up the receiver. "Hello?" There was sleepy irritation in her voice.

"Are you always so charming in the morning?" Deke's voice was tinged with cheerful sarcasm and served to bring her the rest of the way to wakefulness.

"What do you want, Deke?" Her tone hadn't changed.

"Well, maybe first of all, some sympathy for my

shattered eardrum. What did you do—throw the phone?"

"No," she mumbled guiltily. "It dropped on the floor when I reached for it."

"That's some consolation, anyway," he chuckled in return. "I hate to be the bearer of bad news, but one of my pilots just called me. There's a chain of bad thunderstorms in the area, and flying could be dangerous. So I had to cancel your flight home."

Shelley groaned. Before she could question him further, she heard the distant rumble of thunder which proved his words. What a disaster. Surely she could get to Butte later in the day. She asked him.

"No doubt the storms will be gone in a few hours, but that'll be too late for your flight. I checked already and there aren't any other flights you could take until tomorrow."

She slumped dejectedly on the floor. "Wonderful. What am I supposed to do?" She spoke more to herself than to him. The thought of spending the entire day and night at the hotel with little more to do than watch television depressed her.

"If I may make a suggestion, why don't you check out of the hotel and come here? At least you wouldn't be confined to a hotel room—and you could spend some time going over the material I have on the Kayalak project. I'm giving a party tonight and you're welcome to attend that and stay here tonight. Then I'll see that you get to Butte in time for your flight tomorrow."

Shelley chewed her lower lip thoughtfully. His suggestion did have its merits, even if it also had some definite drawbacks. She detested the thought of remaining at the hotel and she hadn't brought any work with her. Furthermore, if she were going to prove to herself and to him that she could work with him and not allow personal feelings to get in the way, she might as well start now. Finally she agreed, though without much enthusiasm.

Still, when he showed up later to pick her up, she wondered about the wisdom of her decision. Would she ever be able to see that acutely male figure without experiencing a reluctant attraction toward him? And here she was, agreeing to spend the night as his house guest. Then she abruptly recalled that he had mentioned a party.

"I have nothing to wear to your party," she said aloud, following her thoughts.

He chuckled. "The age-old female complaint." Then he gave her a sidelong glance as he moved out into traffic. "Or am I being chauvinistic again?"

Shelley bit off an acid retort. She was never at her best in the morning, and today was worse than usual. But she made a promise to herself not to start a quarrel and merely asked him to take her to the shop where she had seen the dress the previous evening.

A short while later, she and the dress were back in his car. The dress had fit perfectly, and served to improve her disposition to the point where she was able to carry on a pleasant conversation with him as they drove to his house.

She relaxed even further when, a short time later, he announced his intention of going off to the company club to play handball. He had given her the material on the Kayalak project, and she was settled comfortably in the living room.

He paused before leaving. "The weather has cleared, by the way. You probably didn't notice, but there's a pool out back. Feel free to use it. I'll be back in about an hour and a half."

A pool? Shelley brightened immediately and thanked him. After he left, she laid aside the reports as she thought about swimming. She loved to swim and hadn't been in a pool all summer, since there was none at the ranch. Stepping out through the back door that opened off a corner of the kitchen she found herself on a broad stone terrace, and squinted in the bright sunlight that had replaced the morning's gloom.

To her surprise, the pool was enclosed. It lay at the far end of the house and formed a right angle to the stone façade. The enclosure was mostly glass, steamed up from the moisture created by the warmth of the sun. She saw an entrance, and went across the terrace to it.

Very impressive, she thought as she entered. Perhaps its size was enhanced by being enclosed, but it looked enormous. There were skylights in the roof, which she saw were open, as were many of the glass panels that formed the walls.

Two sides of the pool were surrounded by greenery that grew lush and full in built-in stone planters, and the floor was a striking black and white tile. Several gaily upholstered chaise lounges and matching chairs were scattered about, and a pile of towels was stacked neatly at one end. One obviously used towel was draped over a chair, suggesting that Deke had already gone swimming that day.

Shelley looked about approvingly. She could hardly fault his lifestyle. From what she had seen of the house, he had excellent taste—or at least someone did. It crossed her mind that it was strange he wasn't married. He could scarcely be lacking for candidates.

As she thought about that for a while, she stood uncertainly at the edge of the pool. There was just one problem. She didn't have a swimsuit with her. It was possible that he kept something around for just such emergencies, but he hadn't mentioned it and she had no idea where to look.

Finally the temptation became too strong, and she stripped to her bra and panties rather self-consciously. The beige silk fabric clung to her like a second skin as she slipped in.

The water was a perfect temperature for her. She had never liked cold pools. The pool at the swim and tennis club where she and her mother belonged in Manhattan was always too cold, a concession to the distance swimmers who preferred it that way.

She wondered idly what Jane would think if she could see her now, swimming in the private pool of the man she had condemned so vocally on the phone the day before. Shelley had called her mother for some sympathy after her confrontation with Deke, and she thought now about Jane's remark that, in her opinion, Deke Jordan was not a man to be dismissed lightly. "Velvet covered steel is how I would describe him, dear."

She had paid little attention to the remark at the time, but now she began to see what her mother had meant. Deke had a great deal of charm to him, a smoothness that seemed completely natural—unlike the practiced polish of so many men she had known. But she had caught just a glimpse yesterday in his office of that underlying steeliness. What was she to do about him?

She was still musing about this when she grew tired of swimming and pulled herself out of the pool. Wrapping herself in a big towel, she stretched out on a chaise lounge.

One thought persisted in peeking into her consciousness. She resisted it for a while, but finally gave in and considered it. She had seen a look in those dark eyes that gave her reason to think he found her very attractive. Could she possibly make use of that interest?

Shelley detested women who used their so-called feminine wiles to get something—it ran counter to her feminist beliefs. But, she thought coldly, in a war, any weapon is acceptable. He certainly held a very powerful weapon—that piece of paper that gave him control of her company. So couldn't she justify using whatever weapon she had at her disposal?

But a small voice warned her that she just might get herself into trouble. Her thoughts drifted back to the feelings he had aroused in her, and she suddenly felt very warm. Blaming it on the humid heat of the pool room, she got up, flung off the towel and dove once again into the water.

She swam a few quick laps, then rolled over on her back to float. Did she dare to use his attraction to her as a means of getting Lucky Lady back? Men were certainly capable of making fools of themselves over women sometimes—but was Deke that kind of man?

Shelley had never been in a situation with a man where she hadn't been in control—completely. Even with Michael, she had always known that it was she who set the limits. But comparing Michael with Deke was like comparing a cub to a full-grown lion.

She continued to float in the big pool. She had never had a pool all to herself before, and her makeshift suit felt like a second skin. Sighing happily, she gave herself up to the sensuous pleasure and forgot about her problems for the moment.

"Are you alive, or do I have a beautiful cadaver floating in my pool?" The voice carried over the water as though he were beside her.

Sputtering as she flailed about to roll over and tread water, she spotted him standing near the water's edge.

"You're back early," she said accusingly, embarrassed at having been caught like this.

"No, I'm not. Apparently you've been enjoying yourself." He continued to stand there, not more than six feet away, watching her with an amused expression.

Shelley had become very much aware of the fact that her scanty attire must be obvious to him—and was undoubtedly the source of his amusement. She was embarrassed, but had no intention of letting him see that. Taking a deep breath, she very calmly walked out of the water and up the few steps at the corner of the pool where she had left her towel.

At first she kept her eyes carefully averted from him, but her curiosity got the better of her and, as she bent to pick up the towel, she glanced up at him.

He hadn't moved and neither had his eyes. They were still locked on her, making her all too aware of her vulnerability.

Her anger gave a sharply sarcastic edge to her voice as she wrapped the towel around herself, sarong-style. "Are you enjoying yourself, Deke?"

"I was, yes," he said drily, with an obvious reference to the fact that she was now safely covered by the towel. "But I'm sure you're already well aware of your considerable charms."

Green sparks leaped from her eyes as she glared at him. Was he implying that she had deliberately flaunted herself in front of him? "I'm sorry to have deprived you of your pleasure," she said icily as she unconsciously secured the towel around her breasts.

"You could have stayed in the pool until I left," he pointed out reasonably.

Suddenly his attitude was more than she could take. How dare he assume that she had been deliberately teasing him? She turned away from him contemptuously, but he was too quick for her this time and grabbed her wrist, pulling her roughly against his muscular hardness.

To her dismay, her anger dissipated quickly in the warmth that spread through her from his touch. She caught her breath sharply, staring straight ahead at the dark hairs that curled out of the open-necked shirt he wore.

She tipped her head back and stared at him. A long moment passed, during which she saw his irritation replaced briefly by something else. But then he abruptly let her go and turned to leave.

He paused at the door. "By the way, about the party tonight. Can I trust you to behave, or shall I call it off?"

Shelley stifled the retort she had been about to

make. If he cancelled the party, she would probably be forced to spend the evening alone with him.

"I won't be childish enough to condemn your friends for their poor choice of host."

He nodded, seeming to accept that, and left.

Shelley looked around her at the group assembled in the living room. Perhaps it might have been better if she had been forced to spend the evening alone with him. At least she wouldn't have had to smile and be pleasant to him.

She knew that she should be ashamed of herself. They seemed to be very nice people, for the most part. Her glance rested for a moment on the only one of the guests she didn't like. She had realized very quickly that Sylvia must be Deke's date for the evening, and the woman was making very certain that Shelley didn't forget that fact.

When Sylvia had arrived that evening, Deke had introduced her to Shelley, and told Shelley that she was the owner of the shop where she had purchased her dress. Shelley had been impressed with the shop and had complimented Sylvia quite sincerely. But the response she had received had been no more than coolly polite, and from that moment on, she had treated Shelley like an interloper.

Earlier, when Deke's housekeeper had arrived with her teenage daughter to begin dinner preparations, Shelley had offered to help. Shelley had been told that her help might be needed to get the dinner served. But when she returned to the kitchen just before dinner, she found Sylvia there, issuing orders in peremptory tones. When Shelley saw the housekeeper's disgusted look she was greatly tempted to tell the sophisticated blonde exactly what she thought of her. But she left the kitchen instead, reminding herself that she had promised not to make a scene. Even so, it was probably more from a desire not to embarrass the housekeeper and her daughter than to keep her promise that she walked away.

At dinner, Shelley was seated on one side of Deke, with Sylvia on the other. It very quickly became apparent that Sylvia intended to carry on a personal conversation with Deke that deliberately excluded her. Deke himself seemed oblivious to Sylvia's poor behavior.

At one point, another guest asked Shelley what she did, and Shelley explained about her inheritance. The woman's response to that was an exclamation of surprise that someone so young could assume such heavy responsibilities. Then, glancing at Deke, she said she was sure that he must be a very great help to her with the mining company.

Shelley caught the sudden movement of Deke's silvered head out of the corner of her eye, and knew that he had heard the woman's remark. He had been bent toward Sylvia, talking in low tones, but now straightened quickly.

Shelley allowed an almost excessive amount of time to pass before she responded. Then she turned to Deke with a sweet smile and said that he had indeed been a tremendous help to her. In fact, she didn't know how she could possibly manage without his help. She put just the faintest emphasis on the word "help"—not enough to be noticeable to the others, but enough to be obvious to Deke.

Everyone who heard the remark seemed to accept it at face value, but another quick glance at Deke told her that he had not misunderstood. However, to her dismay, instead of being angry, he seemed merely amused.

The remainder of the evening passed uneventfully, but Shelley was glad when the guests began to leave. The tension of the situation was beginning to take its toll on her. It seemed that no matter how she tried to avoid Deke, he was there. Their eyes met entirely too many times for her comfort and, while she could read nothing in the glances he gave her, she guessed that he was undoubtedly waiting for her to say or do something outrageous.

Also, she had begun to wonder just how much of the dislike she felt toward the blond Sylvia was directed at the woman herself, and how much was the result of her being constantly linked with Deke. Could she actually be jealous? She dismissed the thought immediately.

Shelley had been expecting that Sylvia might linger behind, and she knew that she should excuse herself and leave them alone. However, she was saved from having to make this difficult decision when Sylvia finally left. Deke walked her out to her car, while Shelley went immediately off to bed, wanting to avoid being left alone with him.

But sleep kept eluding her. It was partly the result of an afternoon nap, but she knew it was also because of the tension she felt. Her thoughts began to turn to the pool, and how it had soothed her that afternoon—at least until he had come along to spoil it.

Finally, the urge became too strong to deny. She

crept quietly out of bed and opened her door. Taking a few steps down the hall, she confirmed that his bedroom door was now closed. She thought she had heard him come up earlier. Still, she went back to her room and waited a while longer—just to be sure he was asleep.

Then she slipped into her robe and tiptoed noise-lessly down the hall in the opposite direction from his room. There was a narrow back staircase that led to the kitchen, and from there she went through to the connecting door between the house and pool.

It was a dark, moonless night, and she groped tentatively along the stone wall, trying to locate the light switches. When she found them, she flooded the big room temporarily with light until she found the switch that controlled the underwater lights.

The result was a soft shimmer, not unlike moon-light. She walked to the end of the pool where the steps disappeared down into the water, and shed her robe and nightgown.

The water was deliciously warm and silky against her bare skin, and she quickly gave herself up to the sensuous feel of it as she swam around slowly.

She had just rolled over languorously to float on her back when a noise at the side of the pool drew her attention.

He was clad only in dark slacks, and had halted just inside the door. The shifting lights of the pool caught at and reflected off the silvered hair, making it the only thing she could see clearly of him.

He must have been as surprised to find her here as she was to see him. No doubt he, too, had thought a late night swim to be a good idea. But she began to draw back involuntarily from the water's edge.

"It seems we both had the same idea. Do you mind if I join you?"

Shelley hesitated just a fraction of a second, then replied as casually as she could, "Of course not. It's your pool. And I suppose it's big enough for both of us."

He laughed at that, and she swam quickly away as she saw him reach for the waistband of his slacks. It was only after she heard him hit the water that it occurred to her that it might have been a nice turnabout if she had stayed there to watch him this time.

They both stayed well away from each other, and Shelley was rather amused to think they reminded her of two sharks, circling warily, trying to stake out territory.

Finally satisfied that he was going to stay at his end of the pool, Shelley once again rolled over onto her back and began to float effortlessly.

But as soon as she had begun to drift aimlessly with the ripples, she found she was thinking of him there in the pool with her, also naked. After all, she surmised, if he had been wearing swim trunks, he wouldn't have bothered with trousers.

The thought disturbed her more than she cared to admit. But she reasoned that, after all, she was a normal, healthy female whose sensuous side had been awakened, although not very expertly, she suspected, by her affair with Michael. And, while she could certainly think of some unkind names to call Deke, she could not, in truth, say that he was not a normal, healthy male—no doubt with more experience than she cared to think about.

With two other people, the ending to such an episode might never have been in question. But Shelley wasn't about to take that path. Thinking about using her powers of sexual attraction to gain her way with him and actually putting action to those thoughts were two different matters altogether.

To her consternation, she realized that she preferred to imagine that she could be successful, rather than risk learning that she couldn't control him—or worse still, that she would lose control of herself. For the first time Shelley faced the possibility that a man could gain that kind of power over her.

Disgusted with her thoughts, she told herself that it was only a combination of the powerfully sensuous scene and the fact that he already controlled something that was very important to her.

She had been paying scant attention to where the ripples carried her and suddenly opened her eyes to see that she had drifted much farther than she had thought.

She flipped herself over with agile ease and caught her breath sharply when she saw him treading water only a few feet away.

Time and motion hung suspended in the warm, moist air as they confronted each other. Although neither of them moved, it seemed to Shelley that the gentle lappings of the water were actually urging her toward him. Strange currents ran through the shimmering pool. For a moment she had an almost physical sensation of his body against hers.

With a small involuntary cry she turned sharply and struck out for the steps at the end of the pool. But when she came out of the water, she heard a splash behind her, and knew that he had followed her. Strands of long hair almost blinded her as she groped for a towel—and encountered a sinewy arm.

6

He wrapped the towel around her from behind, and her body was seared by the imprint of his muscular hardness, barely softened by the towel that provided the only barrier between them.

As he began to rub her dry, slowly and gently, a strange languor invaded her, leaving her with a surreal sense of helplessness. Her wet head rested against his hard chest and he moved one hand up to smooth away the wet strands of hair that clung to her neck and shoulders. Firm, cool lips trailed lightly along the sensitive chord of her neck to her bare shoulder. Her body responded so shatteringly to his touch that she stopped breathing for a moment, then exhaled in a soft sigh.

One strong arm tightened about her full breasts, forcing them upwards to spill over from the confines of the towel She felt the cool wetness of his hair as he lowered his head to explore the soft mounds he had exposed

The suddenness of intimacy didn't seem at all strange to her. She gave no thought to the fact that this man was her sworn enemy. At the point when they had faced each other in the pool, they had slipped together into another dimension.

Slowly he turned her to face him and she barely noticed the towel beginning to slip away. Shelley offered no resistance when he claimed her mouth, moving with persuasive pressure to dominate her senses completely.

The elusive towel now covered her only partially, and he slid one long arm beneath it to caress her heated skin, while he held her head imprisoned with one hand.

Shelley was dazzled by senses she had never known she possessed. His tongue entwined itself erotically with hers as he searched out the intimate recesses of her mouth. His strong hands kneaded her pliant flesh until they seemed to be melting together.

She shifted slightly in his arms, straining to get closer to him, and the towel slipped down about her hips. The softness of her breasts was crushed against the hardness of his chest, and her nipples became achingly sensitive as they encountered the mat of curling hair.

"Shelley, I want you." His voice was muffled as he turned his attention to a sensitive earlobe. One hand splayed across her lower back, pressing her to him to make it all too obvious just how much he wanted her.

Shelley felt a thrill run through her that had nothing

at all to do with the sense of power she should have felt. For this was no game of control—she wanted him with a fervency that could not be denied.

The heat that engulfed her left her soft skin burning from his sure touch. She knew she had only to say no and he would release her. But she couldn't bear the thought of such a parting. They had gone too far to turn back now. A primitive need had arisen in her, too, that clamored for satisfaction.

Deke seemed to understand her confused silence and flung away the towel that had just barely covered her. When he bent and scooped her up in his arms, her own arms went instinctively around his neck.

She was deposited gently on the big chaise lounge nearby, and for a moment he loomed over her, a huge shadowy figure, undeniably male. She silently held out her arms to him in open invitation.

Covering her body with his, he began to tease her with small kisses—touching her eyelids, the delicate shells of her ears, the tip of her nose—all the while stroking her yearning body with hands that sought out and found all the intimate pleasure points.

She caught his face in her hands and pulled him to her, tasting the mouth that had teased her so unmercifully. But he escaped once more to trail lightly down across her throat and climb the peak of one soft breast.

His tongue rolled sensuously around a stiffened nipple, and she arched her body to fit more completely against his. Her movement brought a muffled groan from him, as they began to move together in the slow rhythm of building passion.

Finally he raised himself above her, and for a

moment they stared in wonder at each other. She knew that the naked desire she saw in his eyes was mirrored in her own. And she felt the hunger gnawing at her, a hunger that only he could satisfy.

He parted her legs gently, watching her reaction until his own need cried out for satisfaction. Then he merged with her in a fiery drive that tossed them about, until together they reached the zenith they sought.

They remained joined together for a long while, making the soft sounds that only lovers can understand, as their ragged breathing gradually returned to normal and the tremors that shook their slowly separating bodies subsided.

Then he sat up, allowing his eyes to feast on her at length while she lay there, unable to speak or move. He reached out with one hand and ran his fingers lightly over the length of her.

"I think we've found that common ground I mentioned." His voice was soft, and if it hadn't been for the obvious note of wonder she heard, she might have protested. But she knew that what had happened between them had been as startling to him as it had been to her.

She gave a moan of protest as he stood and reached down to scoop her up in powerful arms. "Let's cool off in the pool." He carried her over to the steps and walked down into the water that now seemed very cool indeed.

Slowly he released her, allowing her to stretch to touch bottom. But he kept her close to him and they swam slowly, side by side, until they reached the other end, where he pulled her to him once more. This need to stay close to one another was wonderfully new to her, and she gloried in the feel of his long body entangled with hers, slipping easily through her fingers.

When he finally suggested they swim back to the other end, she shook her head. His lovemaking had left her so weak that she felt she had to cling to him to keep from sinking.

He laughed and quickly levered himself out of the pool. Then he reached down to her and pulled her up with him. Picking her up in his arms once more he carried her back to the other end.

She lay quietly as he rubbed her with a fresh towel, then stood to dry himself. She watched him, growing warmer by the moment as her eyes devoured his naked male body.

Finally he tossed away the towel and reached for her. "Do you have the strength to come to bed, or shall I carry you?" His voice was gently mocking.

A frightening feeling of disorientation was Shelley's first reaction upon awakening. She blinked several times, but otherwise kept very still. Long bristly legs were entangled with hers, and a heavy weight pressed across the hollow of her waist as she lay on her side.

It all came back then with shattering clarity. But for a moment she refused to believe it. Without moving she looked down as far as she could at the long arm that lay across her. Two emotions assaulted her simultaneously: fear and yearning. Fear that she had taken an irrevocable step that would destroy her life, and a yearning to relive those memories that now flashed through her mind.

she went off to the adjoining bathroom, and stood for a very long time in the shower, wondering if she were trying to wash away the memory of his touch on her yearning body.

By the time she had dressed and packed her bag, she knew she was as ready as she would ever be to face him. But when he appeared at the bottom of the wide staircase as she descended, her knees became shaky.

If he was finding this difficult, he was hiding it very well, she decided. To look at him, one would never believe that last night had happened. And she summarily dismissed the impression she had had earlier, that he too had been strongly affected by their love-making.

"Mrs. Thomas has breakfast ready," he said matter-of-factly. "There's time before your flight."

Shelley breathed a sigh of relief that they were no longer alone in the house and silently followed him to the dining room.

But they were alone again, of course, when he drove her to the airport and the silence lay heavily upon them. Once again she was driven to say something, anything, to break it.

"This doesn't change anything, Deke. You do understand that, don't you?" She risked a sidelong glance at him, and saw a muscle twitch slightly along his lean jaw.

"I didn't think it would. As you said, we just got carried away, that's all." He looked briefly away from the road, and their eyes locked upon each other.

It was only a few seconds, but that was all that it

took for Shelley to feel again an unreasonable desire to be held in his arms. She looked away quickly. What was happening to her?

He carried her bag to the small Cessna, where the pilot was waiting for her. After tossing the bag into the rear seat, he turned to give her a hand. This time she accepted his help without thinking. Even the impersonal touch of his hand sent shock waves through her, and she pulled it free as soon as she had gotten into the plane.

He stood framed in the doorway with his dark eyes intent upon her face. Unspoken words seemed to fly between them. But then he began to withdraw.

"Goodbye, Shelley. I'll be in touch."

She merely nodded, too choked up to respond.

7

I told you before, Tom, I don't want to hear anything about it." Shelley's voice held a trace of exasperation as she pushed the papers back across her desk in his direction.

Tom gave a regretful shake of his head. "Shelley, you've made your feelings very plain. But if you ever hope to convince Deke of your ability to run the company on your own, you just can't ignore an important part of its operations."

They had argued off and on about her refusal to get involved in the Kayalak project ever since Shelley's return. But this was the first time Tom had brought forth that particular argument. They had, for the most part, resumed their old relationship—at least to the extent it was possible. While Shelley had in fact forgiven Tom for his part in the deception, she was still very much aware of the fact that he was Deke's source of information regarding her.

She leaned back in her chair, thinking. She knew that Tom was right—at some point, she had to get involved in the Kayalak project. He was also right about something else. Considering it from Deke's point of view, she decided that it must look like a childish tantrum.

Abruptly she reached across the desk and retrieved the papers she had pushed back to Tom. "You're right, Tom. I'll go over these tonight and have Julia make a reservation for me."

Tom got up then, his relief obvious. "Good. We can go over any questions you have on the flight tomorrow."

After he had left her office, Shelley grimaced at the thick report in front of her. But it wasn't really the report that bothered her, of course. Getting involved with the project meant getting involved with Deke again.

True to his word, he had not intruded upon her running of Lucky Lady. There were times when she could almost forget about his control of the company as she made decisions about its operations. But Tom's presence, no matter how helpful it was, served as a constant reminder that Deke could, and probably did, review each and every decision she made.

She had neither seen nor heard from Deke for almost a month now, although Tom's occasional mention of him told her that he had heard from him.

After devoting far too much thought to what had happened, Shelley had decided that, for her at least, their lovemaking had been no more than a natural conclusion to an unlucky coincidence. It had been purely by accident that they'd both ended up in the pool that night, and the sensuality of the scene had simply overwhelmed her common sense.

When she felt like being charitable toward Deke, she would say the same for him. However, when she was in an unhappier frame of mind, she would think that he had quite deliberately seized the opportunity to make her more pliant to his wishes, to show her just how completely he controlled her. At those times, she truly hated him.

Early the next morning she hurried across the windswept airstrip to board the plane, feeling more nervous about this trip than she had about her previous one. At least she looked all business in her tailored beige suit, its severity relieved only by a soft bowtie at the neck of the printed silk shirt.

But her nervousness began to subside as she and Tom began to discuss the report she had read the previous evening. As always, Tom was very helpful, patiently explaining the technical aspects of the project to her. She still had some difficulty, however, in focusing on the matter at hand. She wondered if Tom had told Deke of her last minute decision to come to the meeting.

Several hours later, she received her answer. She felt an unwelcome pang of disappointment when she and Tom entered the conference room at the Jordan headquarters. Deke was not among the men gathered there. But his secretary was present, so she clung to the unwilling hope that he was just late in arriving.

Tom was greeted warmly by all, and saw to it that Shelley was introduced to those she didn't already know. Her presence seemed to create quite a stir among the gathering, so she guessed that none of them had known she was coming.

While Tom lingered with the others, Shelley went off to the small table that had been set up in one corner with a big pot of coffee.

She had just fixed her coffee and turned around when Deke entered the room. Her hand shook as she raised her cup, which she quickly replaced in its saucer. He didn't see her at first and she watched him shake hands with Tom. When he turned from Tom to look sharply around the room, she felt a sudden terrible vulnerability.

His dark gaze found her quickly and he came toward her, as she tried hastily to return to the others. "Shelley, this is a surprise. I had no idea you were coming."

His smile was warmly welcoming, but betrayed no trace of intimacy. She did not return the smile, other than with an ironic twist to her full lips.

"And here I thought you knew everything. I must revise my opinion, Deke." Her voice was tinged with sarcasm.

His smile faded. "Back to square one, I see."

"I wasn't aware that we had ever left it," was her cool response as she brushed past him to take a seat at the big round table, as the others were doing.

Shelley tried to focus her attention on the meeting, with only limited success. Her eyes seemed to be constantly turning to him, even when he wasn't speaking. All too often she would find him watching her speculatively.

Finally, when she thought she could take no more, the meeting broke up. Shelley quickly gathered up her things, intent upon escaping without further contact with him.

But an all-too-familiar hand gripped her arm firmly, and she spun about to face an unsmiling Deke.

"Shelley, before you go, I'd like to speak to you for a few minutes."

She pulled her arm from his grasp, just as he let it go. "We're leaving for Butte now."

A small smile began to tease the corners of his wide mouth. "You won't be leaving for a few minutes. Tom has some business to attend to."

Before she could protest further, he took her arm again, and led her down the hall to his office.

As soon as the door closed behind them, Shelley's temper began to flare. She hated this room, with its reminder of his triumph over her. She had come here before to rid herself of his presence in her life, and here she was again, with no hope of that now.

She stood in the middle of the office, watching him resentfully as he went unhurriedly over to his desk and gestured to a stack of books in one corner.

"Tom tells me that you've gotten a very good grip on the business end of the company already, Shelley —as I guessed you would. But that isn't enough. If you're going to run a mining company, you must learn something about mining itself.

"These texts won't take the place of a degree in mining engineering, but they should at least give you some grasp of the subject. Take them with you and we'll set up regular appointments in the future to discuss them."

She looked scornfully at the books. "Will that be all?"

This time he smiled broadly. "Just about. I wanted to tell you that I'm glad you've decided you can work with Tom again. Being rather familiar with your temper, I was a bit worried about his welfare."

She drew herself up stiffly. "I've forgiven Tom for his part. He was just doing his job." She placed a decided emphasis on Tom's name to be sure he understood just who was being forgiven.

"But, as I said earlier, we're back to square one?"

"As I said earlier, I wasn't aware that we had ever left it." Her voice came out surprisingly cool and collected, considering the memories his words evoked.

As she spoke, he had taken several steps toward her. It was with great effort that she stood her ground. A warm flush began to steal over her but she fought against it.

"Perhaps my memory has failed me but I was under the distinct impression that we had crossed some boundary the last time I saw you." His voice had become seductively soft and she felt her resolve weakening.

"Then your memory has definitely failed you. I haven't changed my mind about you." But her heart was hammering in a suddenly constricted throat. She stared fixedly at the knot in his tie.

"I suppose I'll survive your wrath, Shelley. I must admit that it does have a certain . . . appeal for me."

She was trying to think of an appropriate retort, when he reached out suddenly and drew her to him. The contact with his hard frame brought forth a rush of memories that overwhelmed her and she surrendered easily to his firmly possessive lips.

A tingling sensation reached clear to her toes as he claimed her already parted mouth, moving sensuously over her full lips. Her tongue tried briefly to retreat from his caress, before it too surrendered to his mastery.

One hand pushed aside the jacket, and splayed possessively across the softness of a breast, burning through the thin silk. When her fingers registered the springy touch of his silvered hair, she was shocked to find that they had stopped pushing against his chest, and crept around his neck. But she was immediately awash with shame when it was he who ended the kiss, although he continued to hold her lightly.

"My memory hasn't failed me, Shelley—and neither has yours." There was a husky quality to his voice that made her wonder again about the true nature of his desire to possess her.

"Stay here with me tonight," he said softly as he bent to brush his mouth against the curve of her neck.

"I . . . I can't. We're going back to Butte. Tom and his wife have plans to visit some old friends," she stammered, fighting hard against the urge to accept his invitation.

"Let them go. I'll have you flown to Butte in the morning to catch your plane." He continued to nuzzle her ear, his breath fanning against the sensitive skin.

Taking a deep, steadying breath, she pushed against him, succeeding in creating a small space between them. "No, Deke. Last time was . . . was just an accident. It's not going to happen again."

His arms dropped away from her, the warmth quickly gone from his voice. "I suppose you'll be trying to tell me next that accidents like that have happened to you before."

She felt her face growing very warm and tried to hide it from him. "Of course not, but there's a first time for everything, isn't there?" She snapped the words at him.

He pulled her face back around. "When it happens again, will you still believe it's an accident?"

She pulled away from him once again and quickly turned to leave. "There won't be any second time, Deke. Only fools allow the same accident to happen twice."

Before he could respond to that, she almost ran out of his office. Following the secretary's directions she escaped into the relative security of the ladies' room and stared disgustedly at her reflection in the mirror. Could she possibly believe that the flush on her cheeks and the sparkle in her eyes were the result of an accident?

That evening she was still musing about it as she leafed desultorily through one of the books he had given her. She had forgotten them in her hasty exit from his office, and when his secretary approached her as she and Tom were about to leave, she had at first thought the woman had been sent to summon her back to his office. But then she noticed the books and took them with relief.

Tom grinned at the sight of the titles. "So Deke is

planning to turn you into a mining engineer?'' Shelley merely nodded, thinking that he certainly seemed to be succeeding in turning her into a jellyfish.

Shelley had been invited to join Tom, his wife and their friends for the evening, but she declined, not wishing to intrude into a pleasant reunion for the two couples. So she was left to spend the evening alone in her small hotel room.

Her mood swung between proud triumph that she had refused Deke's invitation and anguish as she thought about what the evening could have been, if she had accepted.

Shelley returned to Mountain Springs more determined than ever to put Deke Jordan out of her mind. Accordingly she was very pleased when she found a message waiting for her that Tony Simmons had called in her absence.

Shelley had met Tony the previous weekend at a party given by a friend of her Denver host and hostess. Finally succumbing to her mother's blandishments about "all work and no play," Shelley had called the sister of one of her close friends in New York. The woman had recently married and was now living with her physician husband in Denver. The call had resulted in an invitation to come to Denver to spend a weekend, and Shelley had accepted eagerly.

Tony had charmed her from the beginning with his suave dark good looks and his teasing manner. It had taken her only a few minutes in Tony's scintillating presence to realize how terribly wrapped up in Lucky Lady and the ranch she had become. She had always been very serious about her work, but her social life in New York had been lighthearted and fun. Now she saw a chance to recapture some of that—and put Deke Jordan out of her mind.

When she called Tony the next day, he reminded her of the invitation she had playfully extended to see her ranch, when he had expressed doubts about its existence. So she promptly invited him to visit her the following weekend.

In the weeks that followed, Tony became a regular visitor to the ranch, which he proclaimed to be a very welcome diversion from the dark-paneled law offices where he was a junior partner. He was rarely serious, but when he was, Shelley learned that he was very unhappy in the prestigious but stuffy law firm.

In his serious moments he showed great interest in Lucky Lady, listening with sympathy to her tales of woe regarding the continued refusal of many of her employees to take her seriously. For some reason known only to herself, she never told him about Deke's control of Lucky Lady.

On one of his visits, she invited Tom and his wife, Jan, to dinner at the ranch. Tony was his most charming self, and he spent quite a lot of time discussing Lucky Lady with Tom, who was also trained in law.

Although Shelley was attracted to Tony, she carefully kept her distance. She didn't quite know why, except that she was sure she wanted no entanglements at this point. She welcomed the attention he paid her, however, and always looked forward to his visits.

For his part, Tony didn't rush her. He made his feelings for her very obvious, but he seemed instinctively to understand her reluctance to become involved. She found, though, that thoughts of Tony didn't intrude into her working life the way that memories of Deke did.

"Tom, it's quitting time," she teased one late afternoon, as she put her head through the connecting doorway between their offices. When he looked up at her, she saw the tired lines on his pleasant face, and realized all of a sudden how very hard he had been working.

After admonishing him not to stay much longer, she left, but on the drive back to the ranch she thought about Tom. He must have had his hands full even before she arrived. Now she had added to his burden by claiming much of his time. Furthermore, Lucky Lady was involved in delicate labor negotiations and constantly being hassled by new government regulations.

It occurred to her that Tom needed help and that she should have seen it before. As the Kayalak project began to take shape, he would have even more work. She wondered, too, although she had never asked, just how much longer Tom would be at Lucky Lady. She recalled Deke's statement that Tom was a valued employee, and suspected that it might not be long. Perhaps the best thing to do was to hire someone now who could step into Tom's position when he departed. She decided to broach the subject with him the next day.

Tony called that evening, and Shelley noted quickly that he lacked some of his usual ebullience. When she questioned him, he admitted that he had been growing more and more restless in his present position and was sending out résumés to other law firms.

However, by the end of their conversation he had cheered up considerably, telling her that the thought of spending the weekend at the Double G had improved his disposition immeasurably.

As she prepared for bed, the day's problems turned over and over in her mind—Tom's heavy burden, Tony's dissatisfaction with his job. A possible solution slowly began to materialize.

"The thought just occurred to me because I know you need help here, Tom, and because Tony called last night and mentioned that he's looking for a job." Shelley defended her suggestion to a surprised Tom the next day.

"Besides," she continued, warming to the idea, "his family was in the mining business at one time. I don't know if he told you that, but he seems to know a lot about mining. And he's trained in law, just as you are."

Tom looked at her thoughtfully. "You're right about my needing help, Shelley. And more than that, we have to think about the future. I won't always be here, you know."

Shelley nodded wistfully. She couldn't bear to think of Tom's leaving, although she knew he would at some point. At times like this, she quite forgot his connection with Deke, and thought only of how she would miss him.

Tom continued, interrupting her thoughts. "Give me some time to think about how the responsibilities could be divided Then we can talk about it some more "

She agreed, but brought up the matter tentatively to Tony that weekend.

"Me work for Lucky Lady?" He looked very surprised. "It hadn't occurred to me. But I'm not sure I could."

Shelley frowned at him. "Why not?"

He grinned suddenly, wiping out the serious look he had given her. "Don't look so serious. I just meant that I'm not sure I could work for you. Falling in love with the boss isn't supposed to be a good idea."

Shelley flushed warmly, but felt a prickly unease. She really didn't want to hear such things. But she didn't push him away when he reached over to take her hand tenderly.

"Shelley, you're driving me up the wall, do you know that? I know you won't talk about him, but whoever he is, I sure wish you'd get him out of your mind."

She looked away from him, not wanting him to see the pain that she knew must be in her eyes now. "I will, Tony, but I need more time."

He kissed her then, and she was reminded of Michael's kisses—smooth and practiced. But something was missing. She hadn't realized it with Michael, but since her relationship with Michael, Deke Jordan had been thrust into her life. When Tony finally released her, she was left with the horrifying thought that nothing would ever be the same again.

Later, as she tossed and turned in her bed, she determined that she would get over Deke. She just needed more time, as she had told Tony.

8

~~~~~~~~~~~~~~~

Shelley stifled a yawn, then nervously smoothed down the skirt of her soft green jersey dress. She had gotten little sleep the previous night and the day stretched far too long ahead of her.

She had such mixed feelings about this trip. The opportunity to see Alaska excited her. But the knowledge that she would be seeing Deke again dampened her enthusiasm. And it hadn't been thoughts of Alaska that had kept her awake last night. Her only consolation lay in the fact that they wouldn't be alone.

Tom had first approached her about the proposed trip two weeks ago. Deke had decided that he wanted a first-hand report on the progress at Kayalak, and had invited Shelley, Tom and Lucky Lady's chief engineer to join his party. They would meet the Jordan group in Butte and fly by chartered jet to Fairbanks, where they would spend the night before flying still further north to Kayalak.

Shelley had spoken with Deke just once since their last meeting. He had called to apologize for not having kept his promise to set up regular appointments to discuss the mining texts. She had replied coolly that she understood that he was very busy, and that she was working her way through them and getting some help from her chief engineer. She did not allow the conversation to stray into personal matters, and noted with some chagrin that he made no attempt to do so.

Perhaps, she thought as they landed in Butte, he's willing to let our relationship remain on a purely business basis. But a nagging doubt remained that they could carry it off.

Shelley and the two men went immediately to the Learjet that would carry them to Fairbanks, and she unconsciously began to seek out Deke's tall form. But she couldn't find him, even when they were told to fasten their seat belts. Her curiosity got the better of her and she asked Tom where he was.

Tom jerked a thumb toward the cockpit. "Up there. He's thinking of buying one of these and he wants to try it out. So he's flying copilot."

Shelley sat back in her seat, not knowing whether she was relieved or not. At least he was out of sight for the time being.

They had been airborne for some time, and Shelley was listening to Tom and Ben Thomas, Lucky Lady's chief engineer, discuss a problem with one of their mines. She still understood very little about the technical aspects of mining, but she had at least learned enough from Deke's books to be able to ask intelligent questions.

She was about to query them on one point, when she glanced up to see Deke's tall form huddled over before her. It was just barely possible for her to stand upright in the plane, and his extra height forced him to stoop.

Tom was the first to greet him and ask what he thought so far about the Learjet. Shelley was slightly amused with his boyish enthusiasm and couldn't help smiling at the sight.

"Boys and their toys, Shelley?" Deke turned his attention to her suddenly, as he caught her smile.

"Something like that," she admitted, unable to wipe away the smile.

He arched one dark brow at her. "I think I'd have to call that sexist. Wouldn't you agree?"

His taunt brought a chuckle from Tom and a flush to Shelley's cheeks. But he left them to talk for a moment with one of his staff, preventing Shelley from having to find a suitable response.

The flight continued without incident. After they landed in Fairbanks, they were driven to their hotel. So much for the "frontier" image, Shelley thought, as she looked out at a typical city landscape, complete with high rises.

A meeting was being held shortly after their arrival, and Shelley walked into the room where it was to be held to find Tom there, with two young Jordan engineers. She was introduced to them and learned that they were assigned to the Fairbanks field office of Jordan. Both of them looked at her as though a dull meeting suddenly showed some prospects of improving.

She was deep in conversation with the two men, asking questions about life in Alaska, when Deke came in with the others. Was it her imagination or did he actually seem annoyed to see her with the two engineers? She filed the thought away for future consideration.

The meeting convened, and Shelley followed the proceedings as closely as she could, quite deliberately keeping her gaze away from Deke. Instead she found herself catching the eyes of the two engineers more than once. At one point, when Jordan's chief engineer was discoursing at length on some particularly obscure point, Shelley caught an exaggerated, long-suffering look on one of the engineer's faces.

She smiled involuntarily and then turned to catch Deke's disapproving frown. For just a moment she felt like a schoolgirl caught talking in class. But she merely gave him a blandly uncomprehending look in return and fought the urge to yawn. She had caught some of the infectious lightheartedness of the two young men, and decided that perhaps this trip could be amusing, as well as instructive.

When the meeting finally broke up, the two engineers immediately surrounded her and invited her to join them in the hotel bar for a drink. She accepted and was just leaving when she heard Deke's deep voice calling her.

"Shelley, we have some matters to discuss. Could we meet upstairs?"

Shelley became slightly peeved at the order masked

as a question and said coolly, "We have two hours until dinner. I'll meet you in half an hour."

She exited quickly with the two men but not before she had the satisfaction of seeing an irritated look on Deke's face. As they walked toward the bar, one engineer began to kid the other about being on the boss's blacklist. When they had seated themselves at a small table, Shelley asked what he meant.

"We've been told that The Man considers us too frivolous," the blond young man grinned. "I can't imagine why."

After the laughter subsided, she asked them about Deke.

"Oh, he's brilliant. No doubt about it. There isn't anything he doesn't know about mining. And Jordan is a good company. But he's a real slave driver who expects everyone else to work as hard as he does. We're up here on our own and he doesn't like it. For some reason he seems to think we don't work very hard."

More laughter followed that remark, and then the other engineer spoke up. "Everyone keeps hoping that he'll get married one of these days and have something else to occupy his mind."

Shelley felt a chill. "Is he planning to get married?" Images of the detested Sylvia came into sharp focus.

Her companion gave an exaggerated sigh. "Not that I know of. I personally think he's already married —to the company."

The other man gave her a speculative look. "Was it my imagination or don't you two get along very well?"

Shelley felt uncomfortable, but tried to make her

response light. "We're only business associates. He was a friend of my father's. I really don't know him very well." She surprised herself with the glibness of her tongue. But she felt herself growing very warm at the thought of just how well she did know their boss

It was past the appointed time when she got up and excused herself to go up for her meeting with Deke. She assumed that he intended to go over some of the texts she had been studying, and had brought along her list of questions with that in mind. As she left the bar, she saw that all of the others had congregated there, too. Deke would be waiting for her in the suite.

Taking a deep breath, she opened the door to the suite to find him alone, as she had guessed. He was sprawled on the sofa, papers spread about him, with his feet resting on the coffee table.

He looked up as she entered, then quickly organized his papers and stuffed them into an attaché case.

"Would you like a drink, Shelley?" He stood up and went toward the bar in one corner.

She declined and sat down stiffly on one end of the sofa. He fixed a drink for himself, then took a seat on the other end. Even when she knew that he was watching her as he sipped at his drink, she kept her silence. It crossed her mind that he seemed ill at ease.

"Shelley, Tom tells me that you're considering hiring someone to assist him." He broke the silence that was growing uncomfortable.

Shelley nodded, relieved to discuss something impersonal. "Yes. Tom is overworked. And besides, I know he won't be staying forever. It would be good to have someone there to replace him."

Deke leaned forward to concentrate on the glass he held. When he spoke, he did not look up. "I agree with that. But Tom tells me you have someone in mind for the position."

It was then that Shelley began to feel the first faint prickles of unease. To cover it, she said, too brightly, "Yes, I know of someone who may be interested and would be perfect for the job. Tom has met him."

Still he didn't look at her, although she turned to face him. "Yes, I know. He won't work out, Shelley."

Shelley was too stunned to become angry at that moment. "What are you talking about, Deke? You can't mean Tony?"

And then he did look up, his dark eyes full of regret. It was echoed in his voice. "I'm sorry, Shelley, but I am talking about Tony. He lied to you. He's not an attorney—he never finished law school. And his family was never in the mining business. My guess is that he learned just enough to fool you in that regard."

"How could you possibly know all this?" There was a tight edge to her voice, and she gripped the arm of the sofa as she continued to stare at him.

"I had him checked out when Tom said you seemed intent on hiring him."

Suddenly unable to sit still any longer, she jumped off the sofa and whirled about to face him. "That was underhanded of you, Deke. I thought we were through with all that."

He said nothing for a long moment, while he drained his glass. Then he looked directly at her. "Are you in love with him?"

The question took her by surprise, and it was a few

seconds before she could choke out a reply. "That's none of your damned business, Deke."

"Perhaps not," he said tightly, "but if you are, there's something else you should know." He paused, and looked at his glass, then got up and went back to the bar.

"And what is that?" she asked scornfully, glaring at his broad back.

"He's married." He didn't bother to turn toward her.

Waves of shock ripped through her and her throat grew painfully dry. She had no doubt that he was telling her the truth, even though she would have liked to disbelieve him. Dear charming Tony. While he was spending weekends at the ranch with her, he had a wife waiting for him at home. Suddenly she hated all men. But at the moment, she hated Deke even more than Tony.

"Damn you, Deke Jordan. It was because of you and your overbearing ways that I got involved with Tony in the first place. He took my mind off you." She ended in a choking sob, sinking back down on the sofa. Her words rang in her ears. Why had she said that? She lowered her head and covered her face with her hands.

But she flinched when his arms gripped her shoulders. She raised her tear-stained face to find him kneeling before her.

"Shelley, I'm sorry. I had hoped you weren't in love with him." She heard the genuine regret in his voice, but pushed him away violently.

"I'm not in love with him. And we weren't having

an affair. But I hate you for your meddling, Deke. It's been that way from the beginning. Can't you understand that all I want is for you to stay out of my life?" She glared at him and saw a muscle tighten along the firm jaw, as he straightened up to stand before her.

"I can't do that, Shelley." His tone told her quite clearly that he wished he could.

Unable to bear his presence any longer, she got shakily to her feet and walked across the room to the privacy of her own room. Once there, she stumbled over to the bed and flung herself down.

She was so tormented by her thoughts that it took a while before she realized that what bothered her most was not what she had learned about Tony, but Deke's attitude toward her.

That he considered her a burden to be borne for the sake of his friendship with her father was all too apparent. But what became equally apparent was that she was in love with him. The shock of it brought her sharply upright in the bed.

When had it happened? She had told herself—and him—that she hated him, but in fact she was in love with him. She began to understand the old saw about love and hate being two sides of the same coin. She still hated his control of her company but she loved the man.

It was clear that she was no more than a promise to be kept—to her dead father. He wanted out and she, who proclaimed loudly that she wanted him out of her life, in fact didn't.

She didn't know how much time passed before she became aware of voices in the lounge. A quick glance at her travel alarm told her that they were gathering for drinks before dinner. She would have to face them—and Deke.

She pulled herself off the bed and went into the bathroom to repair the damage done by her tears. That accomplished, she changed into an ivory wool suit with a full skirt and short jacket, accented by a bright blue silk shirt. Nights were cool up here, even in the summer, and the jacket would come in handy. A quick glance in the mirror assured her that she looked considerably more together than she felt at the moment.

She was firmly resolved that Deke wouldn't see her pain, lest he guess the truth. She had come all too close to letting him know, and she wasn't about to let it happen again.

Deke stayed well away from her in the lounge and at dinner at a nearby restaurant. Since the two young engineers had joined her, however, she was kept well occupied. She found herself feeling very grateful for their company this evening.

After dinner, everyone gravitated to the lounge once more. Shelley considered excusing herself to go to bed, since she was tired but her two companions cajoled her into letting them take her on a tour of Fairbanks night life.

Deke was standing nearby when she accepted the invitation. "Shelley, we're leaving very early in the morning."

She stiffened at his paternal tone. And all the anger and frustration she felt suddenly poured forth. She gave him a saccharine smile.

"Don't worry, Daddy. I'll be home early." She turned abruptly to join her two friends, but not before she saw, with considerable satisfaction, the deep crimson flush that crept over his rugged features.

As soon as they were out in the hallway, one of her companions whistled appreciatively. "Wow, Shelley. You've got some nerve. I've never seen anyone get to The Man like that."

Shelley just smiled.

"Go away," she mumbled, burying her face in the fluffy pillow. But she instinctively recognized the hands that were shaking her none too gently. She sat up, instantaneously awake and angry.

"What do you want, Deke? I'm tired, and I don't want to talk to you now. How did you get in here anyway?"

His face came slowly into focus, and she noted the grim set of his wide mouth.

"We're leaving in one hour, Shelley. And I got in here because you didn't lock your door." His tone was as unpleasant as his look.

She frowned. She was sure she had locked the door. But then she remembered the other door, the one that led from the lounge. What was he saying about leaving in one hour? She concentrated on the travel alarm beside her bed. He was right. She had forgotten to set it. She slumped back to the pillow, forgetting for the moment his presence in her room.

But she was brought sharply back to reality by his cold anger. "Shelley, your remark last night was completely uncalled for. You can say anything you like to me when we're alone, but I won't stand for that kind of rudeness in front of my employees."

Shelley couldn't resist a little smile at the recollection of his embarrassment. But she quickly saw that he was in no mood to appreciate humor. "You asked for it, Deke."

"All I did was remind you of our early departure—with good reason, as you can see."

His sarcasm wiped away any remnants of her good humor. "I don't need a father, Deke. I've managed all my life without one."

"Then perhaps that's exactly why you do need one. But I'm not applying for the job, believe me." His dark gaze swept over her disheveled form.

"You could have fooled me," she grumbled at him. "You meddle in my life, tell me to come home early—doesn't that sound like a father to you? It certainly does to me."

His grim features relaxed suddenly into a smile, as his eyes roamed over her upturned face and down to where the deep vee of her nightgown barely concealed full breasts.

"Maybe I do sound like one sometimes, Shelley, but I don't feel very fatherly toward you. Except for the times when I'm tempted to turn you over my knee."

Now it was Shelley who could not see the humor in the conversation. "If you ever try, so help me, I'll knock you flat, Deke Jordan," she hissed at him.

His smile merely broadened. "That I'd like to see."

His amusement at her expense tipped her volatile emotions into the danger zone, and she rose quickly to her knees in the bed. He sat down beside her and before she quite knew what had happened, she was being held securely in his lap. A tiny strangled cry escaped her lips as she felt her body responding to his closeness. A big hand splayed itself across her bare back, and beneath her, she could feel the hard thighs.

When she looked up and saw the reluctant desire in his eyes, he was already lowering his face to hers, and she trembled in anticipation. Their lips met just as she clutched at the taut muscles where his neck joined his broad shoulders, and she was lost in tumultuous sensations as his mouth tasted hers and his hands roved restlessly over her scantily clad form.

As he moved away from her mouth to caress her throat, he lowered her slowly back to the bed, covering her with his exciting maleness.

The thin straps of her gown were quickly slid down so that he could fondle the softness beneath, and she gasped her pleasure as his tongue rolled sensuously across the already sensitive nipple, teasing it, surrounding it—while he rubbed a thumb gently over its twin.

Shelley shifted herself to fit more completely to him and reacted with a breathtaking rush of desire when she felt him press demandingly against her. But then he raised his head, glancing away from her for a second. He straightened up quickly and looked down at her regretfully.

"There isn't time now, Shelley. We have to leave soon." He moved toward the door, raking his fingers through the hair she had mussed with her groping hands. "Get ready and I'll have some breakfast sent up to you."

As her breathing slowly returned to normal and her pounding heart quieted, she grew angry once more. She had seen the look of regret in his eyes, but his maddening self-control was what she remembered.

9

~~~~~~~~~~~~~~

Shelley was determined to stay as far away as possible from Deke for the remainder of the trip. She managed to maneuver herself into the plane that he was not piloting, since the size of the group and the landing strip restrictions demanded that they take two smaller planes to the mine site.

With him out of sight, if not out of mind, she settled down to watch the scenery. It was a clear day, and they flew at low altitudes over the frozen tundra. Thick clusters of pines grew along the hillsides, the open land was spotted with rocky outcroppings and patches of snow. She looked in vain for the animal life that she knew inhabited this hostile environment. The guidebooks she had picked up in Fairbanks mentioned elk and caribou among others, but there was nothing to be seen in the endless stretch of barren wilderness.

As they flew over the shining ribbon of the Yukon River, Shelley thought about the state's sobriquet: "America's Last Frontier." It occurred to her that it would probably be called that hundreds of years from now and seemed to her to be a strangely timeless land that could never be tamed.

The trip was a long one but they finally went into a wide arc and the pilot, a Jordan engineer, said they would circle until the other craft landed. Shelley looked down at the tilted world beneath her and frowned. There was no sign of civilization. Finally she saw a rambling building or group of buildings, but that was all. They were infinitesimally small in an area where the landscape was frozen into wrinkled brown shapes.

Then they landed and she climbed out of the plane. The sense of vastness that she had felt when flying over this land was increased tenfold on the ground. She could almost feel herself shrinking to the insignificance of a pinpoint.

She stopped for a moment, aware that Tom had stopped also, near her. "It's frightening," she murmured without turning toward him.

"Yes," was his almost whispered response. She knew it was Tom's first trip here, too.

And then they turned toward each other and began to laugh at their hushed comments. A cold wind hurried them along to join the others at the two Jeeps that awaited them. Shelley was glad to be wearing her heaviest pair of corduroys, a thick wool sweater and her bright green down ski vest.

A short trip in the Jeeps brought them to the collection of buildings she had seen from the air.

Actually there was only one long low building that rambled over the uneven terrain, connected by zigzagging corridors. Off to one side was a small cabin perched on a rocky outcropping.

In response to her surprised question, Tom told her that this was all there was. Office, living quarters, communications center, work areas and the mine entrance were all in one building, to facilitate work in often inclement conditions. The only other man-made structure in sight was a tall tower springing up from the highest of the hills behind the building.

As she stared up at it, Tom followed her gaze. "That's not a TV tower, by the way. Radio is their only connection with the outside world—and it isn't always dependable."

Shelley shook her head in amazement when Tom ventured the further information that the mine was more than a hundred miles from the nearest town, over dirt roads that were impassable most of the year.

She and Tom followed the others into the building and went into a large room that was apparently a dining room and recreation area. A pleasant aroma drifted in from somewhere to remind her that she had eaten little of the breakfast Deke had ordered for her.

Then her eyes met his briefly and he beckoned her over to him. Reluctantly she threaded her way through the group to him, and he introduced her to a weather-beaten, white-haired man who turned out to be the project supervisor. He looked very much as though he belonged to this hostile land, but his blue eyes twinkled pleasantly.

"A pleasure, Miss Grant. I never expected to be welcoming a lady to Kayalak, and certainly not such a beautiful one." He gripped her hand in his big gnarled one, and she realized just how out of place she was here.

A short meeting followed, during which Scotty, the supervisor, gave them a brief rundown on the situation. Kayalak was an old mine, opened during the great gold rush in Alaska almost a hundred years ago. It had produced much gold for a short while, but then had been abandoned, as the cost of getting the gold out exceeded its value.

Shelley had learned from Tom that Jordan had acquired title to the mine some years ago when they had bought another company. Until recent technological advances in mining engineering and the increased prices being paid for gold combined to make Kayalak appealing, it had lain untouched.

With an optimistic geological and engineering report, Deke had decided to reopen the mine. Actual mining would not begin here for some time. The crew on hand at the mine were highly skilled men—geologists, engineers, explosive experts and equipment operators. All equipment had to be flown in, which created problems. But still the work was proceeding on schedule, as Scotty pointed out proudly.

As Scotty answered some questions, Shelley glanced about the room and began to wonder about sleeping arrangements. Her attention was drawn back to the supervisor when he suggested that they all settle in, then return here for lunch.

The others moved back toward the doorway to collect their bags and Shelley trailed uncertainly behind. She saw them pick up their bags and disappear down one of the corridors. Deke remained behind, and she saw that he held her bag as well as his own. A sinking feeling had come over her even before he spoke.

"We're staying at the cabin. The accommodations down here aren't exactly suitable for a woman."

Shelley eyed him warily. "That explains why I'm staying at the cabin. But why are you staying there?"

He gave her an unfathomable look before replying with a slight smile. "Rank has its privileges," he remarked. "I don't like to sleep in single beds."

He turned and began to walk away, carrying their bags. Shelley stared after him wordlessly. The cabin hadn't looked large enough to have two bedrooms. Her common sense surfaced, though, even as something else stirred within her. From what she knew of Deke Jordan, it appeared highly unlikely that he would flaunt an affair with her before his staff and hers. She willed her feet to move and caught up with him just as he turned to see if she was following.

"This is Scotty's cabin, by the way. But he'll bunk with the men tonight. It's not luxurious, but you'll be a lot more comfortable here." He spoke over his shoulder as they entered the cabin.

Shelley almost smiled at that remark. As if she could ever be comfortable in his presence. She looked anxiously about the cabin. There was one large room that apparently served as a living room, dining area and office, since there was a desk in one corner.

He crossed the room in long strides. "This is your room," he said, and dropped her bag just inside a small bedroom that contained a single bed.

"Where are you going to sleep?" she asked, hating the slight breathlessness in her voice.

He seemed not to have noticed her trepidation as he waved an arm toward the other side of the room. "In the other bedroom."

A short while later they were back in the main building, sitting down to a hearty lunch, at which they were joined by the mine crew. Shelley had conjured up images of seal meat or bear stew but was pleasantly surprised to find the fare quite good, although a bit much for her. There were thick sandwiches of beef or ham, and a good hearty soup.

After lunch, hard hats were handed out. Shelley's covered her eyes and occasioned some good-natured teasing from the men, until she piled her thick hair on top of her head and succeeded in raising it a bit.

Then they were escorted through a series of tortuous corridors to the mine entrance. The elevator was a large metal cage which could easily hold fifty men. Shelley followed the others into it reluctantly. She had not as yet been down in a mine. Tom had suggested a tour several times but she had kept putting it off. Her sole excursion underground had been to the Luray Caverns in Virginia, during a vacation with Jane some years ago. She hadn't liked it much, despite the beauty of the caves.

After what seemed an interminable descent, they stepped out into the wide main shaft where an acrid smell greeted them. Shelley sniffed questioningly and Tom explained that there had been blasting that morning. Shelley had already developed a great respect for the experts who could blast beneath the earth without bringing their world down around their ears, but she was still nervous about it.

As Scotty was talking to Deke and several of the

others, Shelley wandered off to one of the smaller shafts that bisected the main one. Scotty had said that traces of gold were still to be seen in this older part of the mine. She walked tentatively up to a dark, damp wall, looking for some evidence of the precious metal.

Seeing nothing, she tilted her head back and looked up at the ceiling of the shaft. The voices of the others floated eerily in from the main shaft, echoing off the walls. Water dripped all around her.

And then something began to happen to her. As she stared in the semidarkness, she could see in her mind's eye the untold tons of earth above her. She began to feel it pressing down upon her and her breathing grew labored. She looked down, but to no avail. Now the walls seemed to be converging upon her. She could no longer hear the ghostly voices, although she briefly thought she heard murmurs.

Shelley strove to calm herself but panic took over. She began to run blindly, intending to find the others.

From far away she heard someone call her name. She tried to answer, but nothing would come out. And then she heard her name being called again and running steps behind her. By the time Deke had caught up with her, she had run deeper into the shaft, where puddles and debris had slowed her down.

"Shelley, stop. It's all right. You're safe." He quickly wrapped his long arms around her.

Slowly the panic passed, as she leaned against him to still her trembling body. Other voices were echoing down the narrow corridor, and Deke shouted that she was all right. By the time the others had reached her, she had calmed down enough to be angry—at herself this time.

Scotty suggested that she get back to the surface and the suggestion was seconded by Tom. But Shelley shook her head defiantly. "I'm fine now. I don't really know what happened. I just panicked."

"Scotty's right, Shelley. You're going up." Deke's voice was quiet but firm.

She turned her anger on him. "So you can have one more example of my incompetence. No, thank you."

Before Deke could respond, Scotty intervened. "Miss Grant, many people, including mine owners, panic down here. Some get over it, but others never do. And the only cure I know is to get your feet on the surface and the sky over your head."

"Scotty's right, Shelley. I'll go back up with you." Tom's placating tone inserted itself.

"I'll take her back up, Tom. You haven't been here before, and I have." Deke put a firm hand against her back, and Shelley gave in, rather than create a further scene. She felt defeated and embarrassed.

She stayed as far away from Deke as possible in the big cage and not a word passed between them. When they reached the top, Deke suggested they go outside for a few minutes, following Scotty's "cure."

Seeing the broad expanse of blue sky lifted the lingering burden from her almost immediately. She breathed deeply of the cold air, paying no attention to Deke's presence.

"Shelley, for a normally self-confident woman, you sometimes show an amazing lack of it. Why should I think you incompetent because of something over which you have no control?"

She turned on him, hands belligerently pressed

against her hips. "Why?" She glared at him. "Because you would seize upon any excuse to believe that I'm incapable of running a mining company."

He looked down at her silently, then shrugged his wide shoulders and turned back to the building. "Have it your way. I'm going back down."

That evening Shelley sat before a blazing fire in Scotty's cabin. Deke had remained behind to play poker with some of the others. Shelley had been invited to join them, but had declined the invitation smilingly, telling them that she was about as good a poker player as she was a miner. Thankfully, she had been able to join in the laughter that followed.

She opened the book that Scotty had recommended to her, when he had showed her the equipment used to extract the gold from surrounding rock. She found it interesting, but her mind kept wandering back to the episode in the mine.

She had been wrong to treat Deke the way she had. But how could she possibly explain to him that it was the result of terribly conflicting emotions? She loved him—but she resented his control of Lucky Lady more each day. It just got in the way. In the way of what? she thought sadly. He didn't return her feelings. Oh, he wanted her all right, no doubt as badly as she wanted him. But he didn't love her and never would. A tear trickled down her cheek before she could wipe it away, and she turned determinedly back to the book.

He came in a few minutes later and quickly settled down to work at the desk in the far corner. Shelley had her back to him and didn't turn to greet him.

Finally she could stand it no longer. It wouldn't change his feelings the way she wanted him to, but she had to apologize to him. Slowly she got out of the big chair and went over to him.

He heard her approach and looked up warily from his work.

She gave him a tentative smile. "Deke, I'm sorry about the way I acted this afternoon. Thank you for your help."

The tension drained quickly from his face. He leaned back in the swivel chair, smiling at her in that slow way that she found so beautiful. "Apology accepted. I think you were angrier with yourself than with me. You're far too hard on yourself, Shelley."

Her eyes widened in surprise. She recalled their first meeting, when he had seemed to read her mind. It was a discomfiting thought.

She looked away from him for a moment. "I know I expect a lot of myself. Maybe too much. But I get so frustrated when everyone around me knows more than I do. At the ranch, there's Jud. And at Lucky Lady, there's Tom and all the others. And you." She turned back to him.

"Shelley, you're learning. Give it time." His voice was gentle and something deep inside responded frighteningly to that gentleness.

"I guess you're right," she murmured and turned back to her chair.

But she grew tired before long and couldn't concentrate on the book, so she announced her intention to go to bed and received a mumbled good night from Deke, who was still bent over his work.

She had fallen asleep quickly, but was jolted awake by a scream. By the time she knew that it was she who had screamed, the bedroom door had been flung open, and light from the other room poured in, silhouetting Deke's large form.

She sat up in bed, realizing that she was trembling and suddenly recalling the nightmare. He came over and sat down on the edge of the bed.

"Bad dream?" He brushed away the tendrils of hair that partially obscured her face.

She nodded, remembering some of the dream. She had been down in the mine again. This time the ceiling had actually begun to fall upon her—in slow motion.

He stood up and she realized that she must not have slept long, since he was still fully dressed. "Will you try some whiskey? That's all I can offer, but it might help."

She wrinkled her nose in distaste. "I don't like whiskey, but maybe it will help."

He returned quickly with a glass and she drained the contents rapidly, drinking it like medicine. Then she sank back onto the pillows once more.

She didn't sleep long. Again she awoke to the sound of her own scream, shivering with fright as the dream repeated itself. This time it seemed she could taste dirt in her mouth as she awoke from the terror of the cave-in.

Once again he was there. But this time she could barely see him in the subdued light from the other room. She murmured sleepily that she was sorry and shook her head to free herself from the grogginess brought on by tiredness and the effects of the whiskey.

143

Before she could sort out her thoughts, he had pulled the covers from her. She felt his muscular arms beneath her, as he lifted her from the bed. She made a weak, vague sort of protest as he carried her from the room.

"If this is going to continue, at least I won't have to get out of bed." He strode quickly through the big room to his bedroom.

Only when he dropped her onto the other bed did her thoughts coalesce to make her aware of where she was. But she was too cold and tired to protest, so she snuggled quickly into the warmth of the bed, only slightly alarmed as he got in on the other side.

She did not awaken again until daylight was peeking around the edge of the curtains. Deke was lying on his back, with one arm wrapped about her as she curled next to him. Her head rested on his chest, a hard but pleasant pillow.

Her rational mind told her to get out of bed while she still could, but her body resisted separating from him. When he awoke, she knew it was too late. He murmured a sleepy good morning to her, and she felt his lips brush against the top of her head.

As she raised her head, she wondered if she could claim that this was an accident, too. Twice now, the force of circumstances had flung them together—into a situation she suspected neither of them could control.

His lips trailed lightly down across her forehead as he tightened his grip on her and shifted to lie on his side. When his mouth came to rest against her own, their lips met tentatively at first, until he slowly increased the pressure, and began to tease her hesitant tongue. They lay facing each other, kissing and touching, for a long while.

Then, finally, he moved a fraction of an inch from her, and said in a husky voice, "Shelley, do you want me?"

She almost laughed at the absurdity of it, but merely nodded as she clasped his head and pulled him to her again. Their scanty clothing vanished a moment later, and they resumed the slow exploration of each other. She gloried in the feel of him—hardness and unexpected softness, sinewy muscle and bristly hair.

His mouth sought the swelling softness of her breasts, tasting her taut nipples. Then he lifted her above him, burying his silvered head in the valley between her breasts as his hands circled her waist. His tongue flicked erotically against the sensitive skin.

Shelley burned with a need for him and moved her body against him to ease her longing. She felt his answering desire, and moaned softly.

Longing turned quickly to demand when he lowered her once again to the sheets and raised himself above her. He groaned her name over and over as he came to her, filling her with his need and encouraging her with soft words and strong hands to meet his desire with her own. They floated together, joined by a passion that conquered them both.

Afterward they lay side by side, as he continued to stroke her softly with warm hands that kneaded her sated flesh.

Shelley wanted to seize the moment and hold it forever. But reality was crashing in upon them, as the wonder of their lovemaking began slowly, painfully, to evaporate. His silence was enervating, when there was so much she wanted to hear from those lips that had aroused her to such peaks of ecstasy.

They both jumped as the alarm clock beside the bed shrilled loudly. Whatever lingering tenderness still remained was banished by its summons.

10

⌒⌒⌒⌒⌒⌒⌒⌒⌒

Mr. Jordan is here, Miss Grant." Julia's pleasant voice startled her as it spoke from the intercom.

She had been dreading this appointment ever since Julia had informed her a week ago that Deke's secretary had called. In what had been the only conversation between them after that morning in the cabin, Deke had promised he would set up an appointment to discuss the mining books she'd been reading.

Shelley still burned with embarrassment as she recalled the scene. Since they had separated into the same groups as before for the early morning flight back to Fairbanks, she had not been on his plane. Upon their arrival there, he had once again copiloted the Learjet for the return trip to Butte. Then, finally, at the airport in Butte, he had approached her.

She didn't know what she had been expecting, except that she wanted some indication that their lovemaking had affected him, too. But she had been sadly disappointed. He had told her only about the promised sessions on the texts.

Her reaction to his all-business demeanor had been a purely defensive one—she withdrew into a shell of cold propriety. The carefully maintained façade had failed to crumble even under his brief but intense scrutiny. She had spent the rest of the day and evening locked in her hotel room, pleading a headache, while in fact she suffered from severe heartache.

Deke certainly had been in no rush to see her again, she thought despairingly. Almost a month had passed since the trip to Kayalak. And his appearance now was, of course, strictly business, yet another reminder that she and her company were his responsibility.

She had not told Julia to send him in, a foolish gesture, since she was as prepared to see him as she would ever be. Getting up slowly from her chair, she walked to her office door.

He was talking to Tom, and both men turned toward her. Shelley returned Tom's greeting, but it was to the taller man that her eyes were drawn involuntarily. She wondered how she could ever have thought she might get over him. The effect he had on her was of an overwhelming masculinity that sent strange signals to the oft-buried feminine side of her nature. She felt the chaotic responses inside, but carefully preserved a perfectly bland exterior as she greeted him.

"Hello, Deke." She extended her hand to him, but her heart skipped a few beats when he took it in both of his much larger ones, and held it far too long. As they turned to go into her office, she caught a brief, considering look on Tom's face, and it registered unpleasantly in her mind.

Once in the privacy of her office, he lost no time in getting down to business. She felt both relieved and irritated by this, but carefully masked her emotions.

However, as they began to review the texts she had been studying, her irritation gained the upper hand, although it sprang from a different source this time. Initially, as Shelley had begun her studies without Deke's assistance, her chief engineer had been helpful to her. However, as she delved deeper into the intricacies of mining, he began to show a reluctance to enlighten her.

Finally he had said, with a trace of exasperation, "You needn't worry your pretty head about that, Miss Grant," and she had very nearly exploded in rage. Ben Thomas had no idea just how close he came to being fired that day. Only two things stopped her: his tremendous ability and her knowledge that Mountain Springs was his home, and word would get around to her detriment. So she had simply stopped going to him.

She knew that Tom might be able to help her, but he was too overburdened as it was. On this day, as she sat across from Deke, Ben Thomas's dismissal of her "unfeminine interests" still smoldered within her.

She had prepared a list of questions, and they talked for some time—or, rather, he talked and she listened. At one point she interrupted him to ask a question and he paused in his lecture to answer her.

"That's a pretty complex subject, Shelley. I don't

think you're ready for that at this point." He had then gone on with his interrupted lecture.

But the smoldering fire had begun to burn a bit brighter. True, he had not said flat out that she couldn't understand it because she was a woman, but isn't that what he was implying? In her mind, the only difference between Ben Thomas and Deke Jordan was that the latter knew better than to use the chauvinistic words of the former.

She stayed quiet for a while, but finally ventured another question, almost daring him to dismiss this one. But to her surprise and perhaps disappointment, he got up from his chair.

"We could discuss this better by looking over some of the maps."

She too got up and glanced out the window at leaden skies that reflected her mood. Then, shaking herself loose from her dismal thoughts, she followed him to the dreary windowless room where all the Lucky Lady's maps were kept.

A short while later, she was lost in a fascinating new world. She had always felt an outsider in this room, but now she asked question after question as the arcane lines began to make some sense. Soon she had very nearly forgotten who was responsible for unlocking these mysteries for her.

She was reminded very quickly, however, when he dropped an arm casually about her shoulders as he leaned over to point out something on the map spread before her. That casual touch sent shock waves through her, and she very rapidly became aware of their isolation in the small room. She was disgusted with herself for her failure to maintain a purely business relationship, hoping fervently that he hadn't noticed.

She turned to ask him a question, just as he leaned forward from his place behind her, and they stared at each other from the very intimate distance of four inches. She felt his arm tighten around her shoulders and opened her mouth to say something, when the door behind them opened and Tom appeared.

They both turned to face him, and Shelley saw once more that faintly surprised look on his face. Deke made no attempt to remove his arm, so she moved as far from him as she could, without being too obvious. Things were difficult enough as it was, and she certainly didn't want Tom to get any ideas.

"I thought I'd better warn you two about the white stuff," Tom said with a rueful smile.

"White stuff?" Shelley repeated his words questioningly.

Deke straightened up and frowned. "The forecast said flurries. I checked at the airport when I flew in."

Tom shrugged. "Well, there are about two inches of 'flurries' on the ground already and eight more expected. Also, the wind has picked up and you can't even see to the street." He turned to Shelley. "Everyone's left for the day and you'd better be getting along yourself, Shelley, before the road to the ranch gets too bad."

"Damn." Deke swore in exasperation. "I was planning to fly back to Denver in time to catch a plane to California tonight. But I guess I'd better check on motel accommodations."

Shelley glanced at him, then turned to Tom. "Isn't the motel closed?" She knew the town had only one motel.

Tom nodded. "George usually takes his vacation just before the ski season. He won't be open until the end of next week." Mountain Springs wasn't a ski resort, but its one motel did pick up the overflow from the big resorts some distance away.

Tom turned once again to Deke. "You're welcome to stay with us, if you don't mind the living room sofa. My sister and her kids are visiting, and the place is a madhouse."

Shelley felt a sinking sensation. She was trapped. There was no way she could get out of inviting Deke to stay at the ranch.

"That won't be necessary, Tom. Deke is welcome to stay at the ranch. I'll just go call Mrs. Jackson." She got up and returned to her office, where she stared in amazement at the world outside. Tom had been right—she couldn't even see the street.

She called the housekeeper to alert her to the arrival of an overnight guest and, stuffing some papers into her attaché case, was just about to pull on her boots when Deke returned to her office.

A few moments later they stepped out into a blindingly white world with blustery winds that very nearly knocked Shelley off her feet and forced her to accept the support of Deke's arm.

"Let me help you around to the other side," he said as they approached her car.

If he had offered to drive, she just might have accepted, since she knew that she was inexperienced at driving in snow, especially in the big sedan she had inherited from her father. But his assumption that she would want him to drive aroused her wrath. Perversely she determined to drive herself.

"Since I'm driving, I'll get in on this side," she told him tightly. "And I assume you can get around to the other side without my help." She couldn't resist the last thrust and turned to see his reaction.

For a moment she was sure he would protest, and was disappointed when he didn't. As she got into the car, she wondered why she always seemed to be spoiling for a fight when he was around.

The big car slid a bit in the unplowed lot, but Shelley found the going much easier when she reached the street. She drove slowly and carefully, mindful of the fact that the big sedan was almost too much for her to handle under the best of circumstances. She had begun to feel slightly more comfortable as they reached the outskirts of town. The car was handling well, and she silently thanked Jud for having put on the snow tires the weekend before. She had kidded him at the time that he was rushing the season a bit, but he had reminded her—prophetically, as it turned out—that winter came early in the Rockies.

She cast a brief sidelong glance at her passenger. He filled entirely too much of the car, as he sat there in his tan shearling jacket. And she wondered why he had acquiesced so easily. But then her attention was drawn sharply back to the road, as the traveling became more difficult.

Vicious winds tugged at the car, with visibility near zero in the failing light and driving snow. Great waves of white powder blew over the tops of snow fencing erected along the edge of the road. The landscape took on a hostile, unfamiliar look.

She slowed the car to a crawl, forcing herself to relax when she realized that she had a death grip on the wheel. She almost missed the turnoff onto the secondary road that led to the ranch. The going was much more difficult now, as she realized that the main road must have been plowed.

Shelley was busy calculating just how much distance and how many obstacles lay between them and the ranch, when she came upon a curve that had never attracted her notice before. Suddenly, in the middle of the curve, there were headlights glaring at her. Since she had no idea where she was on the narrow road, she instinctively pulled the wheel to the right to avoid the oncoming vehicle, which she now saw to be a pickup truck.

The surprised and frightened cry that echoed through the big car was hers, although she didn't recognize it at first. The car swerved, narrowly missing the oncoming truck, then skidded wildly as she desperately applied the brakes.

In a daze, she heard Deke's muffled curse as they came to a jolting stop against the steep bank alongside the road. The car was tilted at a precarious angle, apparently caught in a ditch at the base of the bank.

"Are you all right?" She turned quickly at the sound of his voice, then nodded mutely. She stared down at her hands that were still gripping the wheel tightly.

A tap on the window startled her, and she recoiled in surprise when a face stared in at her, as Deke reached across to depress the window button.

"You folks okay?" A leathery face peered in at them.

"We're fine, but I'd appreciate a hand getting out of here. It looks like we're in a ditch." Deke spoke across her, as she sat silently, staring at nothing.

"Glad to help. You're John Grant's girl, aren't you? I recognized the car." The man peered once again at her.

Shelley nodded, still unable to speak. In her mind, they were still spinning out of control across the road. Deke's hand gripped her shoulder.

"Get into the back, Shelley. I can't get out on my side."

Numbly she did as told, accepting his help to climb clumsily into the back, where she huddled miserably in a corner while Deke clambered into the driver's seat.

Within a few minutes they were back on the road, thanks to the efforts of the two men from the truck and Deke's driving skills. Shelley was numb with shock She knew they had come within inches of hitting the truck, and it had been all her fault. Why had she insisted upon driving? What was it about Deke Jordan that seemed to drive her to such ridiculous lengths? She could have injured them both, not to mention the men in the pickup.

As they continued slowly but surely to the ranch, she waited for his outburst. But it never came. She saw him glance in the rearview mirror several times, but she didn't acknowledge it. Yet how easily she now accepted his control of the situation, even though the road grew steadily worse. She glared resentfully at his gray head.

Finally they were home. She got out of the car

before he could come around to help her, and discovered that her legs were rubbery. She brushed past his helping hand and barely heard Mrs. Jackson's greeting. She stopped only when she had reached the bottom of the staircase.

Turning to Deke she said, "I'm sure you could use a drink. Help yourself. I'm going up to change." She practically ran up the stairs, but not before she saw the grim look on his face.

She lingered as long as she could, changing into jeans and a pale blue cashmere sweater. From her window she could see her car pull away and assumed he must be taking it to the garage on the far side of the house.

Finally she forced herself to go back downstairs, but instead of seeking him out, she went to the kitchen to find that, as usual, Mrs. Jackson had everything under control.

Jud was there, too. He frequently ate at the house, since they discussed ranch business over dinner. He got to his feet as she came in, his weather-roughened face relaxing into a smile. "I understand that you decided to try your hand at winter driving tonight."

Shelley blushed. "I . . . I didn't know it would be so bad."

"From now on, I suggest you let me chauffeur you when the weather is bad. And you should consider getting a smaller car, one a woman could handle better."

She nodded. Why could she accept this from Jud, but not from Deke? "Did I do any damage to the car?"

Jud shrugged. "I didn't see it. I met Deke as he was

coming back to the house. But he said there's just a small dent. Nothing serious. It could have been a lot worse." He fixed a sober gaze on her.

"I know." She shivered as she recalled the sickening speed with which she had lost control. "Maybe we could go car shopping this weekend. I'll need your help, Jud. I don't know much about cars." There it was again. She had no hesitation about asking for his help—and admitting her own inadequacies. She was confused. Leaving the two of them in the kitchen, she steeled herself for the confrontation to come and went to the living room.

He had his back to her, as he fixed himself a drink at the portable bar in the corner. But he heard her. Turning slightly to acknowledge her presence, he asked her what she'd like to drink.

There were still grim lines around his wide mouth as he handed her the drink, before sitting down beside her on the sofa. The silence between them lengthened until she could stand it no longer.

"Well, say it, Deke," she finally blurted out. "Tell me how stupid and childish I was, to have insisted upon driving."

When she finally turned to face him, she saw his face relax into a smile for the first time since they left her office. "It seems I won't have to bother, since you're doing a very good job of it without my help."

Shelley flung herself off the sofa and began to pace the room, drink in hand. "You and your damned superior attitude. You drive me to do things that I know are foolish." Immediately she began to regret her candor.

"I was just thinking the same thing about myself," he replied calmly, peering at her over the rim of his upraised glass.

"Wh–what do you mean?" she stammered in perplexity.

"I've been wondering why I let you drive in the first place," he said quietly.

"It's my car," she bristled.

"True enough," he replied evenly. "But I knew you wouldn't be able to handle it."

"Because I'm a woman." She hurled the words at him.

"Because you grew up in a city where few people do much driving. As to your being a woman, I'm not so sure about that, either. Some of the time you seem to me to be no more than a spoiled little girl."

Shelley flushed angrily. "I'm sure your definition of a woman is some helpless little creature who's just overwhelmed by your masculinity. Like dear little Sylvia." She regretted her final words immediately and bit her lower lip in frustration.

He laughed. "At least dear little Sylvia would have had enough sense not to drive in that snowstorm."

She was incensed. "Why is it men can only feel like men when they're surrounded by silly, clinging females?"

He cocked his handsome head to one side, regarding her with a crooked grin. "There are times when I wonder just how much you do know about men, Shelley. My guess is that you've scared them all away with that prickly attitude of yours."

"Unfortunately I haven't scared them *all* away—you're still here." She smiled sarcastically at him.

"That's because I don't scare so easily. And because I always did enjoy a challenge." As he spoke he stood up, making her feel entirely too small.

The only sound in the room was the ticking of the grandfather's clock in the corner, as they stared at each other. But just as he made a move toward her, Jud appeared in the doorway to call them to dinner.

Shelley breathed a heartfelt sigh of relief as she preceded the two men to the dining room. Conversation at dinner was mostly between Deke and Jud. As soon as the meal was over, she dragged Jud off to the office to go over some ranch business.

After lingering as long as she could with Jud, she let him go, and heard him say good night to Deke, who must have returned to the living room. Still, she remained in the office, going over figures, and working on things that were far from pressing. Anything to avoid being with Deke.

Finally Mrs. Jackson appeared in the doorway and asked if there was anything else she needed for the night. Shelley shook her head and bade her a good night, as the older woman went off to her room at the other end of the first floor.

A short while later, Shelley decided to follow her example. Courtesy dictated that she go in to say good night to Deke first, so she went reluctantly to the living room. He was lounging on the sofa, stocking-clad feet propped up on the coffee table as he concentrated on the thick report in his hands. She noted that he made no attempt to get up when she entered the room.

"I'm going to bed now. The snow seems to be letting up, so I suppose we'll have no problem in the morning." Her voice was polite, and no more. "I assume you have everything you need?"

He waited just a shade too long before answering with a glint in his dark eyes that she didn't like at all.

"I'll manage," he said quietly and returned to his work.

Shelley undressed mechanically, her thoughts refusing to stray from the man downstairs. But when she finally crawled into bed, she found that sleep eluded her. She tossed and turned, reliving the accident, then seeing his rugged features floating over her.

Disgusted, she finally got out of bed. Perhaps some hot chocolate would help. She put on her emerald green robe, running the zipper up to the high neckline, and padded softly downstairs. Apparently he was still up, since the living room lights were on. She took care to be quiet as she crept to the kitchen. The hot chocolate was just beginning to steam when she heard a sound and turned to find him standing in the doorway.

She turned away again without a word, pouring the hot chocolate into a mug.

"Having trouble sleeping?" It was a lazy question, as he lounged against the door frame.

"Yes," she finally said, since to deny it would be pointless.

"Some brandy added to that might be helpful," he suggested, as she moved toward him.

"I had already thought of that, but I didn't want to disturb you." She waited until he finally stood aside so that she could brush past him. She was terribly aware of his closeness.

She hesitated at the bottom of the stairs, then went

into the living room and over to the bar, where she poured a small amount of brandy into her mug. He followed her, and poured himself some from the decanter. She knew that she should be taking her mug and going back upstairs, but something held her in place. To cover her indecision, she sipped at the warm aromatic drink.

"You do, you know," he said as he faced her, brandy snifter in hand.

She frowned. "I do what?"

"Disturb me." He raised the glass to his lips, but his eyes never left her.

She thought what a strange admission that was, and knew that she was pleased by it. But she couldn't resist pursuing the matter.

"How do I disturb you, Deke? You seem rather imperturbable to me." She cocked her head to one side, a wry smile on her full lips.

"You know very well how you disturb me. The truth of the matter is that we disturb each other, Shelley, and you've known it at least since that night in my pool—maybe before that. But you'll never admit it, will you?" His voice was softly accusing.

"I don't know what you're talking about, Deke. That was just an . . . accident. Two people caught in circumstances that were conducive to . . ." she faltered, knowing how ridiculous she sounded.

"Conducive to lovemaking," he finished for her. "But how do you explain away the second time, at Kayalak?"

She had to try. "It never would have happened if I hadn't had those nightmares."

"Wrong," he said emphatically. "You were in my

161

bed because of the nightmares. But we didn't make love because of them. I've reached an age where I do find it possible to sleep with a woman without ravishing her, although it might have been difficult in this case. You wanted to, Shelley—as much as I did."

"I did not," she blurted out, knowing it wasn't true.

He laughed. "At least give me credit for knowing when a woman is willing. And you were definitely willing."

"That's not true," she said, repeating her lie. "It just . . . happened."

But he wouldn't let it go. "It happened because you wanted me. Why can't you admit that, Shelley?"

"I despise you, Deke Jordan." She knew her lies were getting out of hand, but there was some strange truth in her words this time.

"No, Shelley, you don't hate me—you hate the control I have over your company." There was calm reason in his voice.

"Have it your way, Deke. I'm tired and I'm going to bed." A sudden return of caution gave impetus to her decision to get away from him.

She began to walk past him, but he caught her by the arm, pulling her to him. She was off balance and clutched at him for support.

"Let me go, Deke." She looked up at him and knew that he could see she didn't mean it.

His mouth closed over hers, softly and persuasively. All her nerve endings went on full alert. He teased a response from her with firm lips that just barely touched hers, before moving on to brush gently against the taut chord of her neck. One hand was tangled in her long hair, while the other reached for the zipper of her robe.

The soft whisper of the zipper being lowered mingled with her low moan as his hand slid inside the open robe, to caress a full breast, barely covered by the thin fabric of her gown.

"Shelley, I want you. And you want me. Stop playing games and admit it." His voice rumbled against her ear.

This time she didn't even try to deny it. Her whole body was crying out her need for him. She thought he surely must hear it.

But he took a half step away from her, waiting to hear her response, still holding her loosely in the circle of his arms. She couldn't bear even that amount of separation.

"Yes, I want you." She finally looked up at him fiercely, as though she expected him not to believe her.

"Well, I'm glad we've finally settled that. For a supposedly liberated woman, you behave suspiciously like an old-fashioned girl sometimes." He softened his words by reaching out to stroke her cheek lightly.

"Being liberated doesn't mean being afraid to be a woman, Shelley, and I think that's what you're afraid of right now." He drew her to him once more and murmured the words against her cheek.

"Let yourself go, lady executive. Let out that soft, sweet person that's hiding inside. I know she's there— I've seen her." He toyed sensuously with an earlobe.

In response, her fingers curled into his thick hair and she drew him to her mouth once more. He stayed only a moment, then swept her into his arms and strode off determinedly to the stairs.

He didn't stop until he reached her bed, where he lowered her onto the mattress, then slid the long robe from her.

"A very sexy nightgown—but I prefer the body beneath." He slipped the straps from her shoulders, and the nightgown, too, was flung to the floor.

She watched as he quickly dispensed with his own clothes, then stood there in all his male glory for a moment, before coming over to sit on the edge of the bed. His dark eyes caught and held hers silently but eloquently, then traveled slowly down the length of her and back again. They left a trail of fire as though he had touched her.

"Deke," she began, not really knowing what she wanted to say. She reached out to touch him and he seized her hand, turning it palm up and running his tongue lightly across the sensitive skin. She found the gesture unbearably erotic and curled against him, trembling as her softness met the bristly hardness of his thigh. Filled with a need to touch him with her lips, she pressed a light kiss against his knee, then rested her head contentedly against his leg.

He reached out to brush away the flame-colored hair that tumbled down over her neck and onto her shoulders, then bent to run his tongue lightly along the curved shell of her ear. All the while his hand played softly over her curves, tracing once more the path that his eyes had followed.

She felt him tense as her hand slid hesitantly along the length of his inner thigh until, with a groan, he moved to stretch out beside her on the bed and clasp her to him. Their lips met once more in an urgent exploration, and hands roamed wonderingly over entwined bodies until she marveled how it could be possible to feel more a part of him than she did at that moment.

Shelley cried out in protest when he moved slightly away from her to roll over onto his back. But he quickly slid a hand beneath her and pulled her on top of him. Her protest turned to a gasp of pure passion as he settled her onto him and she knew that however much a part of him she had felt before, it couldn't compare with the wholeness she experienced now. He bent his knees to cradle her in them, and when she unconsciously tipped back her head, he wrapped a hand about her neck and pulled her back again. Their eyes vied with each other in mirroring the desire that sprang from deep inside, until the rhythm of their joined bodies blinded them both in the all-consuming fiery crescendo that proclaimed their separateness— and their oneness.

They were both still descending slowly from the breathless heights when Shelley, prompted by an unwelcome recollection of the aftermath of their last time together, asked, "What are we going to do, Deke?"

His mouth brushed lightly against her brow, as she lay curled beside him. "Go to sleep, sweetheart. We'll deal with that later."

And she fell asleep almost immediately, murmuring softly as his lips nuzzled against the curve of her neck. There were no regrets in her diffused thoughts and only peace in her dreams.

11

~~~~~~~~~~~~~~

Birthdays were supposed to be happy occasions, Shelley told herself. And this one should be, since two nice things had happened already. First was the surprise arrival last evening of her mother. And then the lovely cake and the rousing, if slightly off-key, rendition of the traditional song by her staff.

But still she stared dejectedly at the half-eaten piece of cake on her desk. She knew she should be grateful for all the people who had remembered and cared. But what she really wanted was presumably far to the north, in his glass-walled office.

She had neither seen nor heard from Deke for weeks now, and the pain gnawed at her constantly. She had awakened that morning at the ranch to find herself alone in bed. At first she had been inclined to believe that their lovemaking had been no more than a particularly vivid dream. But the depression in the empty pillow next to her disproved that.

After she had gotten over her initial disappointment at not finding him there, it had occurred to her that he had simply gone off to the guest room to prevent the staid Mrs. Jackson from finding them together.

So she had gone downstairs, eager to see him again. But something had happened. The lips that brushed lightly against her forehead were devoid of any passion and she could read nothing in the dark eyes. Still, she assumed that the polite conversation over breakfast owed more to Mrs. Jackson's bustling presence than to anything else.

But the formality persisted even when they were alone in her car as she was driving him to the local airstrip. He talked easily, about everything except what she wanted to hear—the answer to the question she had asked the previous night. What were they to do about this powerful attraction that seemed to hold them both in its grip?

No answer was forthcoming, however, as he got quickly out of the car. She opened her door tentatively as he came around to her side, but his mind was already on the condition of the runway and his rented plane. Those lips, so different from the demanding ones whose imprint still lingered on her body, brushed once again across her forehead in an absent goodbye.

"I'll be in touch, Shelley."

And here she was, still waiting. She had alternated between anger and despair, and seeking the only remedy she knew, she had thrown herself headlong into work. She knew there was no logical reason to expect to hear from him this day. It was unlikely that he even knew it was her birthday. But she clung to her irrational hopes.

Because her mother was visiting, Shelley had decided to leave early, and was just clearing off her desk when Julia's voice announced him. She sat stock still, just staring at the intercom device, almost afraid to believe what she was hearing. But finally she asked Julia to send him in. A moment later her office door opened to admit the only birthday present she wanted.

He paused just inside the door, cutting an elegant figure in a three-piece dark suit, and she fought to maintain her composure.

A smile creased the rugged features. "Happy birthday, Shelley. I'm glad I caught you. Julia said Jane is visiting."

She merely nodded, remaining seated at her desk out of fear that her legs wouldn't hold her if she tried to stand. He paused on the other side of her desk, still smiling.

"I have a present for you—two presents, as a matter of fact. But I think this is likely to be the more meaningful of the two." He reached inside the breast pocket of his jacket and withdrew a single folded piece of paper, which he held out to her.

A numbing cold invaded her even before she finally reached out to take the paper from him. Her heart began to pound as she unfolded it with fingers that trembled uncontrollably. It confirmed her worst fears.

"Lucky Lady is all yours now, Shelley. Perhaps it's sooner than John had intended, but somehow I think he would have understood."

Shelley stared for a long time at the paper, then raised her eyes to meet his with the greatest of difficulty. "Why, Deke?" There were many questions in those two words.

He didn't answer immediately, dropping his gaze to the paper on the desk between them. And when he finally did look directly at her, his expression was unreadable. "You've learned a lot in these past months, Shelley. Most importantly, you've learned your own limitations.

"Tom will be returning to Jordan just as soon as his replacement can be found. He already knows about this and agrees with my decision."

"That isn't necessary, Deke. You know I can continue to work with Tom." She was almost pleading. She didn't really understand her sudden fear of losing Tom, but it was there.

"I know you can, but I need him. And you know that both of us will be available to you anytime you need help." He hesitated, then withdrew a slim package from his pocket.

"And before I forget, I have something else for you. I hope you like it."

She was numb by this time and fumbled noticeably with the wrapping. Inside the box was a beautifully wrought gold chain. She picked it up with trembling fingers.

"I had it made up for you out of gold from the Kayalak mine. As you know, they're not really mining there yet, but Scotty managed to get enough to make this."

Shelley swallowed with difficulty, as she allowed the

chain to slip through her fingers. She started visibly as he came around behind her and reached to take it from her.

"Allow me." His fingers brushed softly against the nape of her neck as he struggled with the delicate clasp. She almost cried out from the bittersweet agony of his touch.

But then he had it fastened and drew her out of her chair, turning her to face him. "Very lovely," he murmured, but she didn't notice that his gaze wasn't focused on the chain around her neck.

"Thank you, Deke. I'll always treasure it." She found speaking difficult and stared fixedly at the knot in his tie. But finally she raised her eyes slowly.

The certainty of his kiss sent fire coursing through her body even before his lips touched hers. Quite deliberately she laced her fingers through his hair, to hold him to her. She had to prolong this moment, to make it last forever.

But he finally broke it off, moving a few inches from her mouth. "I must go now, Shelley. I have a plane to catch. Don't hesitate to call if you need me."

And then he was gone, just as suddenly as he had appeared.

Every time she looked at Tom, a lump rose in her throat. She was glad she had presented him with his gift early in the evening, before the sadness of the occasion overwhelmed her.

Shelley was giving a party for Tom at the ranch. It was well attended, an eloquent testimonial to the esteem in which he was held by the employees of

Lucky Lady. He had been truly speechless at the gift, a solid gold horseshoe set at an angle in stone. Both the gold and the stone had come from Lucky Lady's mines, and the gift had been fashioned by a local craftsman.

At the moment the gift served only as a reminder of the golden chain she had received just a month before. Nervously she ran a finger along the necklace that she wore constantly. She alternately cursed herself or congratulated herself for not having invited Deke to the party.

When the last of the guests had gone, she was finally able to erase from her face the smile that she had managed so well all evening. It was ironic, really, that barely six months ago, this would have been the happiest day of her life with Deke Jordan and Tom Roper out of her life, and Lucky Lady all hers.

But instead, all she felt was a bone-deep sense of loss. She would miss Tom in so many ways, but most of all, she knew that his departure severed the last remaining link with Deke.

The weeks that followed saw Shelley plunging herself into a veritable orgy of work. The only way she could deal with the emptiness in her life was to drive herself harder and harder.

Deke called just once, shortly before Shelley left for New York to spend Christmas with Jane. The call was a terrible strain on her. They exchanged the usual seasonal wishes, then talked for a while about business. She tried desperately to feel some warmth in the disembodied voice on the phone, but could hear none.

Only several days later, as she was enroute to New York, did it suddenly occur to her that Deke had seemed uneasy during their conversation. And that seemed very strange. Thanks to an overly friendly seatmate during the flight and a whirlwind of holiday activities in Manhattan, she had had little time to think further about the matter.

But by the time Shelley returned to Mountain Springs just after the New Year, Deke's unusual behavior had been churning in her mind long enough for her to allow herself some small hope. Even his final words began to assume a greater importance to her. It wasn't what he said, actually. For he had only repeated his earlier words, "Don't hesitate to call if you need me." Now that she looked back on it, she had begun to believe there had been a certain desperation in those words. Depending upon her mood at the time, she would either allow herself to hope that there was a hidden meaning, or she would chide herself for having an overly active imagination.

Several times she had almost picked up the phone to call him, with some half-formed notion of forcing him to tell her how he felt. But she never made the call. If he told her that he loved her, what was next? She saw herself being forced to give up her independence, to become only an appendage to him. For Shelley realized that, strong as she was, he was stronger. She just wasn't sure that anything lasting could be built on such a basis.

Finally, one day in late January, the opportunity to see Deke again presented itself. A small mining company in the area was being offered for sale by the family of the recently deceased owner. Jack Tyson, Tom's replacement, was in Shelley's office to discuss the matter. He told Shelley that the heirs were anxious to settle the estate and a quick decision must be made.

Shelley's initial reaction had been negative, but both she and Jack could see some valid reasons to make the acquisition. Finally Jack suggested that they discuss the matter with Tom, and Shelley immediately put through a call to Jordan. But she learned, to her disappointment, that Tom was on vacation in the Caribbean and wasn't expected back for two weeks.

After venturing the opinion that that would be too late, Jack said, "Why don't you discuss it with Deke Jordan, Shelley?"

His surprised expression told her that her reaction had been all too apparent, but she agreed, and then asked Julia to make the appointment.

When Shelley arrived in Jordan two days later, she was in a turmoil. She would tell Deke how she felt and take the consequences. No, she would simply try to gauge his feelings before committing herself. But what would she do if they discovered they were both in love? By the time she reached the Jordan offices, she had begun a list of conditions for marriage to him.

Recognizing the ridiculous turn of her thoughts, she went into a nearby ladies' room, ostensibly to make some necessary repairs to her makeup and hair, but in fact to try to talk some sense into herself. How many times had she imagined this meeting? After they had dispensed with business, she would say quite calmly: "I'm in love with you, Deke Jordan, and I thought you should know that. If you feel the same way about me, then I'm willing to marry you under the following conditions. . . ." The incongruity of it even brought a smile to her face, a rare occurrence these days.

She finally took a deep breath, smoothed down the jacket of the soft gray wool suit she wore, squared her shoulders and marched off to his office.

"Shelley, it's good to see you." He rose from his chair and came to her, reaching out to take her hand in both of his.

He did seem genuinely glad to see her. It took quite a bit of effort for her not to fling herself into his arms and tell him right then. But instead, she managed an outward appearance of calm as she took a seat before his desk. With few preliminaries, she told him about the company that had been offered to Lucky Lady, handing him the information she had brought.

There was silence as he scanned the papers she had given him, while she stared raptly at the silvered head that was bent over the desk. Her fingers actually itched to entwine themselves in the thick, curling hair. When he finished and glanced up, she tore her eyes away, praying that he hadn't seen her expression.

They discussed the matter at some length before Deke glanced at his watch. "I have a meeting in a few minutes, Shelley. There are some things I'd like to check on in connection with the mineral rights the company holds. Let me put someone onto it, and we'll discuss it more this evening."

She nodded mutely. So she was to have yet another chance—in a less formal atmosphere.

"Your secretary asked mine to make a reservation for you at the hotel, but I told her you would be staying with me." He paused and she almost burned under the intensity of his gaze. "We can go out to dinner if you like, or I'll have my housekeeper fix something."

Somehow she found her voice and said that would be fine. She had a sense of things getting out of control. How could she possibly stay in that house with him?

"I'll have someone drive you out to the house now, if you like. You might want to swim. My housekeeper's daughter and her friends may be there, by the way, so you may have some company."

"Y—yes, that's fine. But I didn't bring a suit. I didn't know I'd be staying with you." The thought of the pool nearly choked her.

He laughed and the dark eyes rested mischievously on her. "I seem to recall that problem having arisen before. I doubt if there are any available in the stores now, but you could try."

She nodded once again and finally stood up shakily.

After trying two shops without success, Shelley gave up and told the driver to take her to Deke's house. The big pool was occupied by a gaggle of noisy teenaged girls, so she went instead to the paneled family room and tried to read a novel she had brought along.

But she had managed only a few pages before the housekeeper came down to announce that they were leaving. She put down the book, thoughts of the pool prompting her to look at her watch. It was still fairly early, and he probably wouldn't be home for several hours yet.

A few minutes later, she had peeled off her clothing and was walking down the steps into the pool. She swam for a while, then tried to float. But she couldn't relax, so she turned over to swim some more. Finally she climbed out of the pool and wrapped herself in a large towel. She was tired by now, having slept very little the night before. So she stretched out on the chaise lounge and drifted quickly off to sleep.

She was awakened by a slight sound behind her and swiveled about to see Deke standing in the doorway.

"Were you asleep?" He came over to her, still dressed in a business suit. His voice echoed slightly in the big room, and Shelley was suddenly aware of their isolation.

She nodded sheepishly. "I'm afraid so; I swam so much that I wore myself out, I guess."

His dark eyes took in the securely wrapped towel. "Did you find a suit?"

She very quickly became aware of her scanty covering and reached for the top of the towel involuntarily, as she shook her head. "No. I just waited until the others had gone."

Tension seemed to be crackling through the moist air as their eyes met in unspoken remembrance of another time in this room. Finally Deke began to tug at his tie and announced that he intended to take a swim before dinner.

Shelley swallowed hard. What was she to do? Did he intend to strip right here in front of her? After all, it wasn't as though she had never seen him naked before. But the very thought of it was almost more than she could bear.

With a quick glance at her that left her wondering if her conflicting emotions had shown on her face, he turned and left, saying that he would be back in a few minutes. This was her opportunity to get away, and she knew she should. But her body felt leaden and she didn't move.

A few minutes later he returned, striding to the edge of the pool. She stayed where she was, watching with rapt attention as he took off the blue terry robe he had worn and stood nude for a second, before powerful muscles flexed in a smooth dive into the pool.

Shelley was growing uncomfortably warm in the big towel. That brief glimpse of him had been more than enough to set her pulse racing and make her remember how it felt to be in his arms.

He crossed the pool to the side nearest her in powerful strokes. "Why don't you join me, Shelley?" He was clinging for the moment to the side of the pool, and his wet, curling hair made him look almost boyish.

His invitation seemed to be all that was necessary. She got up slowly, as if in a dream. Fully conscious that his eyes were devouring her, she dropped the towel in a heap at the edge of the pool. All that mattered to her at this moment was that she wanted to be with him. The future could take care of itself.

He backed away from the side, and she dove into the warm water, surfacing just a few feet from him. Desire coursed through her as he moved closer and quickly encircled her with long arms. The water was almost over her head, but he supported her easily as he drew her to him and paused only to smooth away the wet hair from her face before he lowered his mouth to hers.

Water-slicked lips slid smoothly over each other,

even as their slippery bodies met and meshed perfectly. There was a fierceness to his possession of her senses. He held her head imprisoned while his tongue roamed restlessly in the sensitive recesses of her mouth.

She was floating against his rock-hard body and their legs became entangled, causing him to lose his balance. Very slowly they sank beneath the surface, but their lips clung to each other until they were both out of breath.

"What a way to drown," he muttered thickly, as they surfaced, still clinging to each other.

He lifted her higher in the water, so that he could turn his attention to a button-hard nipple. She arched against him as she shuddered from the driving need to have him. Then she felt the side of the pool against her back and his hard male body pressing against her, demanding in its own need.

She wrapped her arms about his shoulders, her fingers gripping the tensed muscles. He murmured her name in a groaning whisper as he spread his hands across her hips and pressed her lower body to him. She gasped with delight when he came to her.

The water quickly grew cool by comparison as their bodies caught fire—a spontaneous combustion that threatened to consume them both. She clung to him, unable to do more than utter small sounds of joy as their bodies slid over one another.

They were still clinging to each other, shivering, after they had met each other's deepest needs. Finally he lifted her out of the pool and quickly levered himself out after her. They dried each other with fluffy towels, taking a very long time as they found each other's bodies wondrous still.

Shelley knew the time had come to tell him how she felt. The words had almost tumbled out during their lovemaking. But as she struggled with the words in her mind, the sudden ringing of the telephone startled them both.

Deke cursed vehemently, but wrapped a towel around his lean middle and went over to answer its shrill summons. After a moment she could tell that it was a business call. Feeling a keen disappointment, she wrapped her towel about her, gathered up her clothing and left him alone.

She went to the guest room where she had left her things and dressed in a silk shirt and form-fitting brown corduroys. She refused to think beyond the moment. All the agonizing thoughts of the past had produced no results, so she decided to let whatever was to happen, happen.

By the time she finally went downstairs, she heard sounds from the kitchen. She walked through the dining room just as he came in, carrying plates and silverware.

"Aren't we domesticated, though? I had no idea." Her full mouth curved in a sardonic smile.

He returned the smile. "Just for that remark, the cleanup afterward is yours. Women are supposed to be good at that kind of thing."

Shelley laughed and never even noticed that he had been baiting her. But despite their banter, she sensed a return of the earlier tension between them. Neither of them spoke of what had just happened between them. Instead, when they sat down before the fire in the family room for a cocktail before dinner, Deke told her that he had gotten the information he had wanted, regarding the company she was considering buying. And she forced herself to pay attention as he outlined his reasons for thinking that she should go ahead with the purchase.

If she had been capable of thinking straight, she might have disagreed with his advice, but she could barely concentrate on what he was saying. She wondered how he could sit there so calmly, behaving as though nothing had happened.

That thought persisted through dinner. By the time she was finishing the after-dinner cleanup, she had grown angry. How dare he turn her world upside down and then act as though they were no more than business associates?

When she had finished in the kitchen, she went reluctantly to join him in the den. He was sitting before the fire, brandy snifter held negligently in one hand. For a moment she just stood quietly behind him, watching him as he stared into the flames, willing him to love her and knowing it was useless. Finally she walked over and seated herself on the boldly patterned rug before the fire, rather than joining him on the sofa.

The question she had been asking herself over and over came out almost involuntarily. "How do you do it, Deke?" She half-turned to him, not wanting to meet his eyes.

His surprise seemed genuine, although she could sense a wariness in his tone. "How do I do what?"

Now she was growing angry once again. "How can

you make love to me like that, and then act as though nothing has happened?" She began to regret her question, but only because she feared the answer.

He regarded her levelly. "And what exactly did happen, Shelley?"

"Wh—what do you mean?" She stammered in her astonishment.

"I mean, did we make love, or was it just another accident, brought on by the circumstances? You said yourself that the atmosphere was responsible the last time." He continued to regard her with maddening calmness as he lifted his glass to his lips.

Shelley knew she was caught in a trap of her own making and remained silent.

"You could say that we're two normal, healthy adults who find each other sexually attractive." He betrayed no emotion as he reached across to the nearby table for the decanter of brandy.

She nodded, pain assailing her as it never had before. She had her answer. But something compelled her to persist. "Is that why you gave Lucky Lady back to me, to prevent any such 'accidents' in the future?"

He nodded slowly, as he swallowed more brandy.

Shelley's head was spinning and she felt tears beginning to burn behind her eyes. All her worst fears had been confirmed. But her pride would not permit her to let him see her pain. With a superhuman effort she willed herself to be calm.

Almost to herself she murmured, "We'll never be able to be just friends, will we?"

But he had heard her. "No, we won't. But I'll still be available to you if you need advice. You know that." His tone was clipped and almost angry.

She knew she had to escape before he saw the tears that were threatening. "Thank you for that, Deke. I think I'll go to bed now." She got up and left the room without another look at him.

Only after she had stripped off her clothes and had gotten into bed did she allow herself the luxury of tears. If only he had been cruel or deceitful, perhaps she could have had the pleasure of hating him now. But he had been honest with her—if brutally so—and she had no reason to hate him.

She lay on her stomach, sobbing uncontrollably into her pillow as she forced herself to relive all the horrible things she had said to him. Torturing herself, she thought about how different it might have been if she had behaved better.

"Shelley, what's wrong?" She jumped nervously at the sound of his voice and rolled over quickly to find him standing beside the bed.

There was no use pretending that nothing was wrong. Besides, she was beyond all deception at this point. So she said, between gulping sobs, "Damn you, Deke. If only you weren't so honest . . . and decent, and . . ." She stopped, knowing she had said too much already.

He sat down on the edge of the bed and drew her to him. The silence was broken only by her muffled sobs as she let him pillow her head against his chest. And the irony of allowing the one who was the source of her pain to comfort her was not lost on her. But whatever the reason, she craved the feeling of his arms about her.

When she had finally calmed down, he set her away

from him. "Finish what you were going to say, Shelley." There was a strange tightness in his voice.

She stared down at the satin quilt that barely covered the rise of her breasts. "You know what I was going to say," she said petulantly. "Don't torment me, Deke, or I'll end up hating you, instead of . . ." She stopped again, and took a ragged breath.

The silence this time was so charged that she finally had to look up at him. What she saw was a look of astonishment.

"Instead of loving me?" The question was asked softly as he finished the sentence for her.

She nodded slowly, amazed that he had apparently never guessed. "I'll get over it," she lied with as much casualness as she could muster. "Anyway, we won't be seeing much of each other in the future."

"I sure as hell hope you don't get over it," was his sudden and vehement reply.

That brought her head up sharply. "Wh—what do you mean?"

He captured her nervously fluttering hand, carried it briefly to his lips, then lowered it to rest with his against his thigh.

"Honey, you misunderstood what I said earlier. I did give Lucky Lady back to you to avoid any 'accidents' in the future. But that didn't mean I didn't want to see you. I just wanted to be sure that our relationship would be free of any problems caused by my controlling your company. That's what I meant when I said that I was sure John would understand. He could never have guessed, and neither did I, that we would get involved with each other.

"I never intended to get involved with you, and each time we made love, I cursed myself afterward for my lack of control. You know, you taught me a lesson that I'm sure you'll appreciate."

"What's that?" she asked huskily.

"I'd always believed being ruled by one's emotions was exclusively a female thing. So I guess you were right to call me a male chauvinist. But it's a mistake I won't make again."

"But why did you wait for me to phone you?" Too much still didn't make sense to her.

"I tried to make it clear that the next move was yours—and it certainly took you long enough." He gave her a look of mock severity.

In her surprise, she had failed to retain her hold on the covers. They slipped away, baring her to his suddenly intent gaze. With a groan, he bent to her, pressing her back against the pillow. After briefly touching her lips, he ran the tip of his tongue slowly down across the hollow of her throat and up to the rosy crest of one breast. Her body was quickly awakened as he teased her with his tongue, then sucked gently on the hardened nipple.

Her body seemed to surge in response and when his mouth began a languorous descent across her rib cage, down to her navel, where he flicked his tongue erotically, she grasped his head and pulled him to a halt.

He looked up at her, puzzled. "No? Honey, don't be frightened. I want all of you."

"I want all of you, too, Deke," she said seriously, "but we may not be talking about the same thing."

A look of dawning realization spread across his face,

and with it came that boyish crooked smile. "Then why don't you ask me to marry you?"

She sat up quickly, staring in astonishment at his face that hovered just above her stomach. "Me ask you?"

He laughed, his warm breath playing sensuously against her sensitive skin. "Isn't that what liberated women do these days?"

"Will you marry me?" It was a question asked in a softly wondrous tone.

"Definitely. It took you long enough to get around to asking. I thought I might have to take matters into my own hands." He sat up and began to pull off his sweater.

"Do you love me?" She almost squeaked the question, her eyes never leaving him as he stood to remove his slacks.

"No, I'm marrying you to regain control of Lucky Lady."

Shelley began to laugh, and didn't stop until he sat down once again on the bed.

"I love you so much that I've been going through hell wondering what to do about it. I haven't even been able to concentrate on my work half the time. Does it make you happy to know that?" He threw the words at her in a pretense of anger.

She laughed throatily, then gasped as he bent his head to resume where he had left off. "Yes. Oh, Deke, I love you so much."

"Not a bad basis for a marriage," he murmured against her.

Much later they were curled against each other in a comfortable silence. And Shelley's thoughts drifted to the future they would share. She propped herself up above him and stared down at his half-closed eyes.

"Deke, what will happen to Lucky Lady and the ranch?"

He opened one eye reluctantly. "We can keep the ranch, and spend as much time there as possible. As to Lucky Lady, it will merge with Jordan Mining."

"And what will I do?" she persisted.

He chuckled lazily, massaging the curve of her hip. "I imagine the merger will keep you busy for a while."

"And after that?" Shelley was not about to be put off so easily.

"After that, I intend to put you on maternity leave." He smiled lazily at her. "Do you suppose we could get some sleep now, or do you want to discuss how many children we'll have, where they'll go to school, and retirement plans?" He pulled her down to rest her head against his chest.

She had been about to protest that she wasn't sure she even wanted children, and she wouldn't give up her career. But she suspected he wasn't going to pay any attention at all—at least not now.

Silhouette Desire
15-Day Trial Offer
A new romance series that explores contemporary relationships in exciting detail

Six Silhouette Desire romances, free for 15 days! We'll send you six new Silhouette Desire romances to look over for 15 days, absolutely free! If you decide not to keep the books, return them and owe nothing.

Six books a month, free home delivery. If you like Silhouette Desire romances as much as we think you will, keep them and return your payment with the invoice. Then we will send you six new books every month to preview, just as soon as they are published. You pay only for the books you decide to keep, and you never pay postage and handling.

YOU'LL BE SWEPT AWAY
WITH SILHOUETTE DESIRE

$1.75 each

1 ☐ CORPORATE AFFAIR
James

2 ☐ LOVE'S SILVER WEB
Monet

3 ☐ WISE FOLLY
Clay

4 ☐ KISS AND TELL
Carey

5 ☐ WHEN LAST WE LOVED
Baker

6 ☐ A FRENCHMAN'S KISS
Mallory

7 ☐ NOT EVEN FOR LOVE
St. Claire

8 ☐ MAKE NO PROMISES
Dee

9 ☐ MOMENT IN TIME
Simms

10 ☐ WHENEVER I LOVE YOU
Smith

$1.95 each

11 ☐ VELVET TOUCH
James

12 ☐ THE COWBOY AND THE
LADY   Palmer

13 ☐ COME BACK, MY LOVE
Wallace

14 ☐ BLANKET OF STARS
Valley

15 ☐ SWEET BONDAGE
Vernon

16 ☐ DREAM COME TRUE
Major

17 ☐ OF PASSION BORN
Simms

18 ☐ SECOND HARVEST
Ross

19 ☐ LOVER IN PURSUIT
James

20 ☐ KING OF DIAMONDS
Allison

21 ☐ LOVE INTHE CHINA SEA
Baker

22 ☐ BITTERSWEET IN BERN
Durant

23 ☐ CONSTANT STRANGER
Sunshine

24 ☐ SHARED MOMENTS
Baxter

25 ☐ RENAISSANCE MAN
James

26 ☐ SEPTEMBER MORNING
Palmer

27 ☐ ON WINGS OF NIGHT
Conrad

28 ☐ PASSIONATE JOURNEY
Lovan

29 ☐ ENCHANTED DESERT
Michelle

30 ☐ PAST FORGETTING
Lind

31 ☐ RECKLESS PASSION
James

32 ☐ YESTERDAY'S DREAMS
Clay

Silhouette Desire

38 ☐ SWEET SERENITY
    Douglass

39 ☐ SHADOW OF BETRAYAL
    Monet

40 ☐ GENTLE CONQUEST
    Mallory

41 ☐ SEDUCTION BY DESIGN
    St. Claire

42 ☐ ASK ME NO SECRETS
    Stewart

43 ☐ A WILD, SWEET MAGIC
    Simms

44 ☐ HEART OVER MIND West

45 ☐ EXPERIMENT IN LOVE Clay

46 ☐ HER GOLDEN EYES Chance

47 ☐ SILVER PROMISES Michelle

48 ☐ DREAM OF THE WEST
    Powers

49 ☐ AFFAIR OF HONOR James

50 ☐ FRIENDS AND LOVERS
    Palmer

51 ☐ SHADOW OF THE
    MOUNTAIN Lind

52 ☐ EMBERS OF THE SUN
    Morgan

53 ☐ WINTER LADY Joyce

54 ☐ IF EVER YOU NEED ME
    Fulford

**LOOK FOR _ALL THE NIGHT LONG_
BY SUZANNE SIMMS
AVAILABLE IN MAY AND
GAMEMASTER BY STEPHANIE JAMES
IN JUNE.**

SILHOUETTE DESIRE, Department SD/6
230 Avenue of the Americas
New York, NY 10020

Please send me the books I have checked above. I am enclosing $_____
please add 50¢ to cover postage and handling. NYS and NYC residents please add
appropriate sales tax.) Send check or money order—no cash or C.O.D.'s please.
Allow six weeks for delivery.

NAME _____

ADDRESS _____

CITY _____ STATE/ZIP _____

Silhouette Desire

Coming Next Month

To Tame The Hunter by Stephanie James

York Sutherland followed Selena Caldwell to the Utah resort, determined to have his revenge. Only this time he met his match: a woman who was just as determined to triumph in love.

Flip Side Of Yesterday by Billie Douglass

Chloe MacDaniel, a geological consultant, and Ross Stephenson, a real estate developer found themselves professional adversaries despite the undeniable electricity that soon was sizzling between them.

No Place For A Woman by Suzanne Michelle

Lamar Steele owner of the Houston Galaxies offered Jessica Brooks a dangerous challenge. But in his arms she fought like a tigress, determined to win, no matter what the rules.

One Night's Deception by Kathryn Mallory

When Natasha Barron locked eyes with Marc Duchaine at a chic Manhattan party, she felt a rush of ecstasy . . . a rush that was present even after he disappeared with a priceless Matisse.

Time Stands Still by Nora Powers

Libby Collins had two passions—one for discovering oil and one for Jared Harper. Now, deep in the Indonesian jungle with Jared as her expedition leader, Libby would have her passions fulfilled.

Between The Lines by Roberta Dennis

Monica left the chill of Chicago for the heat of New Orleans . . . only she had no idea how hot things could get around her new editor Zach Dubois.

Get 6 new
Silhouette Special Editions
every month
for a 15-day FREE trial!

Free Home Delivery, Free Previews, Free Bonus Books.
Silhouette Special Editions are a new kind of romance
novel. These are big, powerful stories that will capture
your imagination. They're longer, with fully developed
characters and intricate plots that will hold you spell-
bound from the first page to the very last.

Each month we will send you six exciting *new*
Silhouette Special Editions, just as soon as they are published. If you enjoy them as much as we think you will,
pay the invoice enclosed with your shipment. **They're
delivered right to your door with never a charge for
postage or handling, and there's no obligation to buy
anything at any time.** To start receiving Silhouette Special
Editions regularly, mail the coupon below today.

Silhouette Special Edition

Silhouette Special Editions® Dept. SESD 7N
120 Brighton Road, Clifton, NJ 07012

Please send me 6 Silhouette Special Editions, absolutely free,
to look over for 15 days. If not delighted, I will return only 5
and owe nothing. **One book is mine free.**

NAME_____

ADDRESS_____

CITY_____

STATE_____ ZIP_____

SIGNATURE_____
(If under 18, parent or guardian must sign.)
This offer expires October 31, 1983

Silhouette Special Editions ® is a registered trademark of Simon & Schuster

READERS' COMMENTS ON SILHOUETTE DESIRES

"Thank you for Silhouette Desires. They are the best thing that has happened to the bookshelves in a long time."

—V.W.*, Knoxville, TN

"Silhouette Desires—wonderful, fantastic—the best romance around."

—H.T.*, Margate, N.J.

"As a writer as well as a reader of romantic fiction, I found DESIREs most refreshingly realistic—and definitely as magical as the love captured on their pages."

—C.M.*, Silver Lake, N.Y.

*names available on request